"We wouldn't be living together in a sexual way. It would be like living in the same apartment complex," Jeb explained.

"I don't think so," Amanda said. "Suppose you have a date and bring her home for the night. What would you do—introduce me as the mother of your child who just happens to live here, but oh please, ignore her?"

Suddenly a flicker of amusement danced in his dark eyes, and it made him even more appealing.

"I haven't had a date I wanted to bring home in a long time."

"That doesn't mean you won't in the future. You're an appealing man," she admitted, "and I suspect women are easily attracted to you, in spite of your not having a date you 'wanted to bring home' lately. That will change."

Silence stretched until she was compelled to look around. He was sitting still as a statue, studying her intently.

"Maybe you and I should try dating."

Dear Reader,

Welcome to the world of Silhouette Desire, where you can indulge yourself every month with romances that can only be described as passionate, powerful and provocative!

The always fabulous Elizabeth Bevarly offers you May's MAN OF THE MONTH, so get ready for *The Temptation of Rory Monahan*. Enjoy reading about a gorgeous professor who falls for a librarian busy reading up on how to catch a man!

The tantalizing Desire miniseries TEXAS CATTLEMAN'S CLUB: LONE STAR JEWELS concludes with *Tycoon Warrior* by Sheri WhiteFeather. A Native American ex-military man reunites with his estranged wife on a secret mission that renews their love.

Popular Peggy Moreland returns to Desire with a romance about a plain-Jane secretary who is in love with her *Millionaire Boss*. The hero-focused miniseries BACHELOR BATTALION by Maureen Child continues with *Prince Charming in Dress Blues,* who's snowbound in a cabin with an unmarried woman about to give birth! *Baby at His Door* by Katherine Garbera features a small-town sheriff, a beautiful stranger and the bundle of love who unites them. And Sara Orwig writes a lovely tale about a couple entering a marriage of convenience in *Cowboy's Secret Child*.

This month, Silhouette is proud to announce we've joined the national campaign "Get Caught Reading" in order to promote reading in the United States. So set a good example, and get caught reading all six of these exhilarating Desire titles!

Enjoy!

Joan Marlow Golan

Joan Marlow Golan
Senior Editor, Silhouette Desire

Please address questions and book requests to:
Silhouette Reader Service
U.S.: 3010 Walden Ave., P.O. Box 1325, Buffalo, NY 14269
Canadian: P.O. Box 609, Fort Erie, Ont. L2A 5X3

Cowboy's Secret Child

SARA ORWIG

Silhouette® Desire

Published by Silhouette Books

America's Publisher of Contemporary Romance

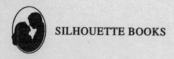 SILHOUETTE BOOKS

ISBN 0-373-76368-9

COWBOY'S SECRET CHILD

Copyright © 2001 by Sara Orwig

This edition published by arrangement with Harlequin Books S.A.

® and TM are trademarks of Harlequin Books S.A., used under license.
Trademarks indicated with ® are registered in the United States Patent
and Trademark Office, the Canadian Trade Marks Office and in other
countries.

Visit Silhouette at www.eHarlequin.com

Printed in U.S.A.

Books by Sara Orwig

Silhouette Desire

Falcon's Lair #938
The Bride's Choice #1019
A Baby for Mommy #1060
Babes in Arms #1094
Her Torrid Temporary Marriage #1125
The Consummate Cowboy #1164
The Cowboy's Seductive Proposal #1192
World's Most Eligible Texan #1346
Cowboy's Secret Child #1368

Silhouette Intimate Moments

Hide in Plain Sight #679
Galahad in Blue Jeans #971

SARA ORWIG

lives with her husband and children in Oklahoma. She has a patient husband who will take her on research trips anywhere, from big cities to old forts. She is an avid collector of Western history books. With a master's degree in English, Sara writes historical romance, mainstream fiction and contemporary romance. Books are beloved treasures that take Sara to magical worlds, and she loves both reading and writing them.

With love to Hannah, Rachel and Ellen…and with special thanks to Debra Robertson, Joan Marlow Golan and Maureen Walters. And to Patricia Smith, my new editor and a wish come true…

One
_____

On a Monday during the first week of June, Jeb Stuart
sat quietly in his car beneath the shade of a tall elm
on a residential street in Dallas. He waited, his calm
manner belying his churning emotions. He glanced at
his watch, and then his gaze returned to the shady
street. Ten minutes later his pulse jumped as a black
car rounded the corner, slowed and turned into the
drive of a small red brick house across the street. He
saw the riot of the driver's red hair before she disappeared up the driveway.

Still waiting, he looked at her surroundings, noting
that she lived in a nice neighborhood. Farther down
the block, sprinklers turned in silvery arcs on lawns.
Her yard had flowers and trees and looked idyllic. In
a few more minutes he was going to disrupt her peaceful life, much like a bomb going off in the neat red
brick house. From all the difficulty he had in locating

her, he guessed that she had expected him to come searching for her and had taken precautions against his ever finding her.

Then the front door opened and another woman came out. From the detective's reports, Jeb knew she was the nanny. Dressed in jeans and a red T-shirt, she sauntered to a parked car, slid inside and drove past Jeb without a glance.

He had waited long enough. He stepped out and crossed the street. With each stride his heartbeat quickened, until it was thudding in anticipation when he climbed the porch steps and rang the doorbell.

The door swung open and only a screen door separated him from the woman he had watched turn into the driveway earlier. Dressed in cutoffs and a blue T-shirt, Amanda Crockett looked up at him and their gazes locked. Jeb stared into wide crystal-green eyes that were enormous and seemed to grow larger. For a moment he was caught and held, but only for a moment, and then he remembered who she was and what she had done.

During the past two months he had rehearsed what he would say when this moment came. Yet now, as he looked down through the screen door into her green eyes, words failed him.

Then he realized it wasn't going to be necessary to say half of what he had intended because all color had drained from her face, and she looked as if she were going to faint.

Fainting would not win her any of his sympathy, he thought, but as he watched, she raised her chin. Even through the screen door, he could see the spark that came into her eyes and he wondered if he was in for a fight. If so, he relished it because he wanted to let her know how much pain she had caused him. He watched her grasp the door, and her knuckles were as white as her face. Had she really thought she could get away with what she had done?

While her world shifted, Amanda Crockett gripped the solid door. As she looked at the tall stranger glaring at her, she could feel the most precious thing in her life slipping away. The moment she had dreaded for three years had come. One look at his face and she knew without a doubt that the stranger before her was the father of her son. In a grown-up version of three-year-old Kevin, she saw the same bone structure, the same straight nose and wide forehead, the same dark eyes and black hair that Kevin had. She knew now how Kevin would look when he was a man.

She tried to get her breath and fight the dizziness that threatened. The stranger hadn't said a word, yet his dark eyes said everything. Determination, anger—there was no mistaking his feelings.

He towered over her, and his broad shoulders were as formidable as his height. Yet it wouldn't have mattered if he had been slender and lightweight—he would have carried the same dreadful threat. More than a threat. The end of her world.

Her stomach constricted as if he had slammed his fist into it, and her head swam. Clutching the door, she gulped deep breaths of air, but words wouldn't come. She had to invite him into her house. From his expression, she knew he would get inside whether or not she invited him, but for Kevin's sake she needed to be civil, even though everything in her screamed to slam the door and run. Grab Kevin and keep running.

"Come in," she whispered.

He opened the screen, and the hinge squeaked as he

swung it wide while she stepped back. When he walked inside, he seemed to fill the hall. Dressed in a white shirt, jeans and western boots, he was rugged and handsome and an overpowering presence.

He turned to face her. "I'm Jeb Stuart. Cherie's ex-husband."

While Amanda fought a knot in her throat, her tears welled up. Nodding, she closed her eyes.

"Are you all right?" he asked gruffly.

"Yes," she said, opening her eyes, thinking he looked as if he would like to lock his hands around her throat and squeeze. She tried to gather her wits and catch her breath, but she failed. She reminded herself that he gave up all rights to his child a long time ago.

Feeling shaky, she closed the door and moved ahead of him. As she ushered him into her small living room, she heard his boot heels scraping the oak hardwood floor.

"Have a seat," she said, perching on the edge of a walnut rocker while he sat on a dark blue wing chair facing her. Looking at him, she became aware that he was very handsome, with riveting dark eyes, sexy, thick lashes, broad shoulders and long legs. When he glanced around the room, she wondered if he thought her home adequate for his son.

She looked at her simple furniture in maroon and navy, her plants, the books on the shelves and the prints that hung on the walls. Kevin's little books were on the oak coffee table. Whether Jeb Stuart liked it or not, this was Kevin's home. She locked her fingers together in her lap while the silence became thick and tense.

"I guess you already know that I'm Amanda Crockett, Cherie's cousin."

"Yes. I've talked with my lawyer and I hired a private detective—that's how I found you."

Amanda struggled against the ridiculous urge to beg him to leave her alone. And then she thought about all Cherie had told her about her ex-husband and anger mixed with fear. She would get her own lawyer; she would fight for Kevin.

"What changed your mind about your son, Mr. Stuart?"

"Changed my mind?" he asked, frowning, a note of incredulity in his voice. She noticed that he gripped the arms of the chair until his knuckles were white. He leaned forward slightly, narrowing the distance between them. "Look, lady, you've got my child. I'm his father and I'm entitled to my son."

"You abandoned him, Mr.—"

"Abandoned!" The word was snapped like the crack of a whip. His face reddened, and even though his voice grew even quieter, it was laced with fury. "I did not abandon my son."

"You may say that now, but at the time—"

"Oh, no," he interrupted, rage blazing deeper in his dark eyes. "I didn't abandon him," he said slowly, with emphasis. "I didn't know Cherie was pregnant with our child. She kept that from me when we got divorced."

Amanda's head reeled again, and the worst of her suspicions were turning out to be the truth. Every word he said was a knife thrust into her heart. Was he lying or telling the truth? If he was lying, he was a good actor. His gaze was direct and his tone held conviction.

Amanda's stomach churned. Deep down she had always wondered if her cousin had lied to her.

"She said you didn't want your child and you left her and joined the army. Where have you been these last three years?"

"I've been in the army," he answered stiffly. "But when I left for the army, I didn't know I had fathered a child. We divorced in October 1997. I haven't seen Cherie since right after our divorce. In January 1998, I went into the army and got out in January of this year. In April I learned about Kevin."

"Who was born the twenty-second of May three years ago." With her anger and fear growing, Amanda wondered who was the truthful one. She knew Cherie wasn't always truthful, but she didn't know whether Jeb Stuart was truthful, either. After all, he married Cherie. What kind of man would marry her cousin? As swiftly as that question came, Amanda knew that most men would be drawn to Cherie.

"Cherie told me that you abandoned her and that you didn't want your child. She didn't want the baby and she knew that I would. She asked me if I would adopt him when he was born. So I went to court and adopted Kevin. I'm his legal mother."

"Legal adoptive mother," Jeb reminded her. "I didn't know about my son. I found out through a friend who knew Cherie and me. Three months after I got out of the army, I just happened to see her. She knew Cherie had been pregnant, but she didn't know Cherie didn't keep the baby."

"Look, I've raised Kevin as my son. You'll tear his life to pieces if you try to take him from me now," Amanda said, growing more certain of the rights she had and angry that he would barge in and expect her to hand over her child.

"Lady, I'm his *father*."

"I have a letter from Cherie saying that you abandoned her when she was pregnant and you knew she was pregnant. Any judge will look at that. I can get Cherie to testify."

"We both know what her testimony is worth!" Jeb's anger surfaced again at the lies Cherie had told.

"You're not going to take my son," Amanda said defiantly.

"Yet you want to keep my son from me," Jeb shot back. He wanted to reach out and shake her and tell her that he had missed his son's babyhood because of her and her cousin.

"Mama?"

At the sound of the soft voice, Jeb turned. A small boy holding a blue blanket stood in the doorway. Dressed in a green T-shirt and jeans, he was barefoot. His thumb was in his mouth.

As Jeb looked at the child standing across the room, he felt as if a fist had clamped around his heart. The rest of the world vanished, leaving only the child. Awe and love and uncertainty filled him. He wanted to touch his child, just touch him. And he saw why Amanda Crockett had recognized him when she opened the door. The resemblance deepened Jeb's awe. This was his son! He wanted to take the boy's hand and say, "I'm your dad, and you're coming home with me," but he knew it was not going to be that simple. The child was wide-eyed, looking from one adult to the other.

"Come here, Kevin. Did you just wake up?"

Amanda's voice was transformed, sounding calm

and sweet and filled with love, carrying so much warmth that Jeb turned to study her before looking back at his son.

Kevin cast a wary eye at Jeb as he scurried across the room to his mother and climbed into her lap to hold tightly to her. While Amanda gently rocked him and stroked his back, Jeb's heart received another blow.

For the past two months, from the moment he had discovered Cherie's deception and the loss of his child, he had been filled with rage and hurt that was compounded when he saw how completely the woman who had his son had vanished. She had left no trail, as though she had known full well that she was doing something underhanded. Now as he watched Kevin wrap his thin little arms around Amanda Crockett's neck, Jeb's pain deepened. For the first time, he wondered how he could take his son from the woman who was truly a mother to him.

She gazed over Kevin's head at Jeb, watching him carefully, and when he looked into her eyes, she gave him a searching stare.

"We need to talk some more," she said quietly, "but we can't right now."

"I can come back," he said, his voice as quiet as hers, yet he knew that her emotions were as much on edge as his. She seemed to think this over, looking down at Kevin, stroking his hair from his face and patting him. Was she a good mother? Jeb wondered.

"If you want to stay for dinner, Kevin goes to bed around eight and we can talk then."

Surprised that she offered dinner, Jeb wondered if she wanted him to see her with Kevin to press her point that she was his mother and they loved each other. She didn't need to, because Jeb could already see they had a close relationship. Was she good to him? he wondered again. Even if she was a marvelous mother, he didn't want to walk out of his son's life and give up all rights.

"Thanks. I'll stay because we do need to talk."

She gave him another one of her cool, level looks, and he experienced a flicker of admiration for her because she had weathered a big shock and was now in control of her emotions and ready to fight for her rights. At the same time, he didn't want to admire her or like her or find her attractive. So far he had succumbed to two out of the three and he wondered whether, if he stayed for dinner, he would also begin to like her.

His anger was transforming into a dull, steady pain, and all his plans for getting his child and watching him grow were going up in smoke. The woman facing him was causing him to readjust his thinking. And, adding to his turmoil, he was too aware that she was damned attractive. His gaze flicked over her in a quick assessment that took in the wild red hair that was an invitation to a man to tangle his fingers in it. His gaze lowered to his son's tiny hand resting against her breast with trust and love. Yet, at the same time, Jeb couldn't keep from noticing the lush fullness of her breasts beneath her clinging blue T-shirt.

"Kevin, this is Mr. Stuart," she said.

Kevin twisted slightly to stare at Jeb.

"Hi, Kevin," Jeb said quietly, feeling another knot in his throat.

Kevin held his small blanket against his face and gazed steadily at Jeb for a long moment until he ducked his head against his mother again. She smoothed his straight black hair. "Sleepy?" she asked him.

He nodded without answering her.

She rocked him slightly, stroking his head while she glanced at Jeb, and he could feel the clash of wills between them. They both wanted the same child. Jeb thought he was entitled to his son, yet for all his young life, the one person Kevin had known as his parent was Amanda Crockett. Jeb realized he was going to have to face that and deal with it in a way that wouldn't cause a lot of pain to his child.

Why had he thought that he could show up and demand his son and she would hand him over? He had expected a fight, but he hadn't stopped to think about her being locked into his son's affections. He had thought of Amanda Crockett as he thought of his ex-wife, Cherie, and Cherie would have given up a child by now. She had given this one up at birth.

"Do you have a grill?" Jeb asked.

"Yes."

"I'll go get some steaks and grill them, and then you won't have to go to so much trouble." He stood, feeling a deep reluctance to leave. He wondered if he would ever get enough of looking at Kevin. What a marvel the child was! His big brown eyes watched Jake solemnly. Oh, how he longed to touch his son, to hold him. "Anything else you'd like?"

"Thank you, no," she answered politely. She stood and picked up Kevin and shifted him to one hip.

As Jeb followed Amanda to the door, his gaze left his son and drifted down over her; he noticed the slight sway of her hips and her long, shapely legs. She opened the door and stepped back for him to leave. When he was outside, he looked back again at Kevin.

"I'll be back in a few minutes," he said. She nodded and closed the door. Jeb felt as if she had slammed it shut on his hopes and dreams.

He shopped quickly, and as he drove back to her house, logic told him she would be there, getting dinner. But his emotions churned and he half expected to come back and find her house empty. Too easily, he could imagine her taking Kevin and running away.

Why hadn't he stopped to think what he would do if she was a wonderful mother to Kevin? Kevin. Jeb liked the name. According to the detective, the child had his adoptive mother's last name, Crockett.

When Jeb returned to her house, her black car was in the drive and relief poured over Jeb. He parked behind it and picked up the sack of groceries. On impulse, he went to the back door and knocked.

She opened it and motioned to him. "Come in."

He entered a kitchen that had mouthwatering smells of hot bread and a blackberry cobbler. He was even more aware of Amanda as she gazed up at him with those compelling crystal-green eyes. Her tangle of red hair and the tiny beads of perspiration dotting her brow gave her a sultry earthiness that was appealing. She blinked, and with a start he realized that he was staring at her. She waved her hand.

"Set the groceries there," she said, motioning toward a space on the countertop. "Kevin isn't into steaks and salad. He gets macaroni."

Jeb placed the grocery sack on the counter and took out the steaks to unwrap them. All the time he worked, he was conscious of Amanda moving around him, of her perfume, of her steady, watchful gaze. She looked at him as though she had invited a monster into her kitchen. Her house was comfortable and appealing, but the kitchen was small, and when he brushed against her accidentally, he was acutely conscious of touching her.

"Sorry," he muttered, glancing at her. She looked up and once more they were caught, gazes locked and sparks that he didn't want to feel igniting. Her lips were rosy and full, a sensuous mouth that conjured up speculation about what it would be like to kiss her. He realized where his thoughts were going and turned away, bumping a chair.

What was the matter with him? He was reacting to her like a sixteen-year-old to a sexy woman, yet Amanda Crockett had done nothing to warrant any blatant male attention. He needed to remember that this woman was tearing up his life and that he was getting ready to tear up hers. If only she would do the right thing, acknowledge that Kevin was his son and simply hand him over. She had no right to take his child from him.

Hope began to flicker that she would be reasonable, realize she had taken a child from his father. Then he glanced across the kitchen into her eyes, which held fire in their depths, and he was certain that wasn't going to happen.

Dinner was a silent, strained event with little conversation by anyone. Jeb began to wonder about his son, who seemed shy and too quiet. Kevin was the only one with an appetite and he ate his macaroni, his bread and butter, and drank his milk.

"You've been in the army?" Amanda asked.

"The Eighty-second Airborne. I was a paratrooper."

She inhaled sharply. For some reason he had a suspicion she didn't approve, yet she probably didn't approve of anything about him.

"Do you and Cherie keep in contact?" he asked.

"Very little," she added, carefully. "I haven't seen her in three years," she said glancing at Kevin, and Jeb wondered if Kevin thought Amanda was his blood mother.

"She's a country-western singer. I've seen her CDs in stores."

"I've seen them, too," Amanda replied, "but I haven't seen Cherie. She's remarried."

"Right, for the third time," he added dryly. "To the actor, Ken Webster."

"You know a lot about her."

"I hired a detective. I got all this information from him." As Jeb talked, only half paying attention to their conversation, he tried to think what he could do about his son. His attention slid back to Kevin. "How old are you, Kevin?" he asked quietly, knowing the answer.

Kevin held up three fingers.

"Three years old. That's getting very big. Do you go to pre-school?"

Kevin shook his head.

"Not yet. He's enrolled for next fall," Amanda said, touching Kevin. She constantly reached out to pat his shoulder or brush his hair from his forehead, and Jeb wondered whether she was affectionate all the time or whether she was giving Kevin attention out of worry now. Jeb leaned back in his chair. He had little appetite, and she didn't seem to have any, either. Yet he was happy to be with Kevin, even though the child seemed inordinately shy.

"Is macaroni your favorite food, Kevin?"

Kevin shook his head while Amanda answered, "His favorite is chocolate ice cream. Maybe chocolate cake is a second favorite and then chicken drumsticks." Her answer was perfunctory, her thoughts still churning.

Glancing over the food on the table, Amanda could hardly eat. What kind of battle lay ahead of her? Was Kevin going to be one of those children she had seen on the television news and in the paper—a child who had two people battling over him while he was always pictured as crying and unhappy?

She was sick at the thought. Every time she looked into Jeb Stuart's brown eyes, she could see his determination, and every time he looked at Kevin, she could see his longing. He wanted his son.

That knowledge tore at her because at the time of Kevin's birth, when Cherie wanted Amanda to take the baby, Cherie had sworn Jeb hadn't wanted his child. Had he had a change of heart or was he telling her the truth—that he really hadn't known? Amanda suspected that he was telling the truth. He looked earnest enough.

She couldn't imagine having one of those horrible battles that hurt Kevin badly. She felt as if Jeb Stuart wanted to cut her heart out and take it with him. She realized he was staring at her, and she guessed he must have asked her a question.

"I'm sorry. What did you say?"

"I see a child's swing in your backyard. Will there be time before Kevin goes to bed to go outside with him and play?"

"Sure," she answered easily. "We're finished. As soon as I clean the kitchen, we'll go outside. Want to?'' she asked Kevin, and he nodded. He started to stand.

"Wait. What do you say?''

"May I be 'scused?''

"Yes, you may,'' she answered, and Kevin slid off his chair and ran to get his toys.

When she stood, Jeb Stuart rose also and picked up dishes. "I can clean up,'' she said.

"This is no trouble,'' he answered politely, and she thought how civil they were being to each other, yet what a sham it was. She knew he was doing it for Kevin's sake, just as she was.

In her small kitchen she could not avoid bumping against Jeb. Each time she was intensely conscious of the physical contact. Every nerve tingled. Jeb Stuart looked full of raw energy, and she wondered if he would make her as nervous if Kevin weren't the connection between them.

Making a rumbling noise like an imaginary motor, Kevin sat on the floor, playing with one of his toy cars. He was so little, too vulnerable. While she watched him, her eyes blurred. She couldn't give up her child! As pain came in waves, she fought a rising panic. Trying to gain control of her emotions, she didn't want to cry in front of Jeb Stuart. *I'm Kevin's legal mother.* But she had seen the pain in Jeb's eyes and she knew he was entitled to his son. She was losing Kevin! She felt queasy, as though she were going to lose the little she had eaten for dinner. She turned on the cold water and ran some over her hand, then patted the back of her neck and her forehead.

"Are you all right?''

His voice was quiet and deep and he was right beside her. She looked up into his inscrutable dark eyes and wondered if they were both headed for dreadful heartache. She feared that no one was going to win in this situation, least of all Kevin.

"I'm all right," she said stiffly, turning to blindly rinse a plate and place it in the dishwasher. A hand closed gently on her wrist. Feeling his touch to her toes, she looked up at him.

"Go outside with Kevin. I'll finish this and join you."

She didn't argue. After drying her hands, she took Kevin's hand and headed outside, thankful to escape her kitchen, which now seemed smaller than ever and filled with the electrifying presence of the most disturbing male she had ever encountered. She still tingled from that casual touch of his hand on her arm. At the kitchen door, she glanced back over her shoulder.

Jeb stood watching her, and the moment their gazes met, another lightning bolt of awareness streaked through her. His midnight eyes were riveting and sexy. She felt a raw edginess around him that she suspected she would have experienced even if Kevin had not been a factor in their relationship. As they gazed at each other, the moment stretched between them, tense, breathtaking, until she turned abruptly. Hurrying outside, she tried to catch her breath and ignore her racing heart.

When Jeb joined them, she was swinging Kevin, and the child was smiling. Jeb stood watching and she was grateful for his patience and caution around Kevin. She knew Kevin was shy, and he became even more withdrawn if someone forced attention on him.

Time seemed to stretch into aeons until they went inside. She bathed Kevin and tucked him into bed.

When she kissed him good-night, she held him close. He hugged her and then lay on his pillow. "Mama, who is Mr. Stuart?"

"He's a friend, Kevin," she answered slowly, wondering how to tell Kevin the truth. *He's your father and he's come to take you from me* ran through her mind while she looked into a pair of dark eyes so much like those of Jeb Stuart.

"I like it better when you don't have a friend here."

"You like it when Megan or Peg come over."

He thought this over and nodded. "I like Megan better than Mr. Stuart."

Amanda merely nodded and hugged Kevin again and fought tears because she didn't want to cry in front of him. As though he sensed something amiss, he clung to her. She kissed him again and tucked him in.

"One more story, please."

She relented and told him another story until his eyes closed and his breathing became deep. Reluctantly, she squared her shoulders, then tiptoed out of Kevin's room and closed the door behind her.

In the small family room, Jeb Stuart stood with his back to her, staring out a darkened window at the night. She knew he was lost in his thoughts because there was nothing to see outside.

"He's asleep."

Jeb turned around and studied her, flicking a swift glance over her that she felt as much as if he had brushed her body with his fingertips.

"Is he always so shy?"

She shrugged and crossed the room to sit down on the sofa, folding her legs beneath her. "He's shy, but he's even more shy with you because he's seldom been around men. He sees me and his nanny, his Sunday school teachers, my friends and, on rare occasions, my aunt, and they're all women.''

She received another assessing gaze. ''You're pretty,'' Jeb said.

''Thank you,'' she answered perfunctorily, because she suspected he was going somewhere with his remark, and her wariness increased. Even as her defenses rose, on another level, she was pleased by his assessment.

''You're too attractive to be single unless there's a good reason. I know this is a blunt question, but you and I are going to have to do some serious talking. Why haven't you married and had your own children?''

She raised her chin. It had been a long time now since she had thought about marriage, and having Kevin had taken most of the sting out of the question, because Kevin had helped her lose a lot of her feelings of inadequacy.

''Why haven't you remarried and had more children?'' she shot back at him.

''I had one unhappy marriage, and I'm not ready to marry again. So back to my question—why haven't you married and had kids of your own?''

Like a lot of other people, she had secrets she didn't care to share. Jeb Stuart's question was personal, and she knew she could refuse to answer him or give him one of the two or three casual replies she had given on dates, but she saw no reason now to be anything except totally honest.

''I can't have children of my own,'' she replied, looking him squarely in the eye, feeling an old familiar pain.

Two

"Sorry. And I'm sorry to pry into your private life."

She nodded, appreciating his apology and fighting an urge to like him. "When I was engaged, my doctor discovered a tumor and I had to have surgery. I'm fine, except I won't ever be able to have children. My fiancé decided that I wasn't really a complete woman, and he broke our engagement."

As Jeb closed his eyes and looked as if he had received a blow, she could guess what was running through his mind. "That was one of the reasons I agreed to adopt Cherie's baby, but it has little to do with why I love Kevin so much now."

"But you'll be much less willing to give him up because of it."

She bristled and swung her legs to the floor, coming to her feet to face him. "I'm not willing to give him up now because he's my son! He's my son as much as if I had given birth to him. I got him when he was a day old. Cherie didn't even want to see him! She hated being pregnant. I love him because he's my baby and has been since he was born!''

Jeb rubbed his forehead. "Lord help us both," he mumbled, hearing her agony and watching tears stream unheeded down her face. He hurt, too, and he couldn't give up his son. "What do you want me to do? Walk out that door and forget that I have a son?''

They stared at each other, and he knew her emotions were as raw as his. She was shaking and white as snow again. She had a smattering of freckles across her nose, and when she became pale they stood out clearly. As she clutched her stomach and ran from the room, he felt as if he had just beaten her.

While he was alone, he paced the room and wondered whether he should just go and try to get back with her later, but that was only putting off what was inevitable. They were each going to have to give or else they would end up hurting Kevin, and Jeb didn't think she would want that any more than he did.

When she returned, she looked even more pale. She moved to the sofa and sat with her feet on the floor. She looked small and hurt and defiant and he felt like a bastard for what he was doing, but he wasn't going to give up his son to save Amanda Crockett's feelings. He pulled a chair to face her and sat down. "We'll have to work something out."

"I don't know anything about you."

"I grew up on a ranch in Saratoga County. I have three brothers—Cameron, a rancher, lives near here with his wife, Stella, on the family land. It's ironic that you left Houston and moved close to my family and home. My brother Selby and his wife, Jan, live in

El Paso. He's with the DEA. The youngest brother, Burke, leads wilderness treks. He and his wife, Alexa, have a home in Houston, so they're not far away.''

"You were a paratrooper, you have a brother with the DEA and another who leads wilderness treks— your family is a little on the wild side.''

He shrugged. "I'm settled now. I bought land southwest of here and I'm raising horses. I hoped to take Kevin there.''

"You weren't a rancher when you were married to Cherie, were you? I thought she told me she had married someone who worked in Houston.''

"I did. As soon as I graduated from Tech, I was hired as a salesman for a Houston feed company. After the second year I was promoted to district superintendent, then in another couple of years, director of marketing. That's when I was married to her. I couldn't have afforded Cherie before then.'' He looked away as if seeing his past, and she wondered if he was lost in memories and talking out loud. "When we met, Cherie was charming, seductive, adorable. As long as she got her way, she stayed charming, but when I quit work and wanted to become a rancher, that's when her true personality emerged. I was wildly in love with her when we married because she seemed to be everything a man could want.''

"I can imagine,'' Amanda said quietly, knowing her beautiful cousin could be delightful as long as things went her way, but when they didn't, she could be dreadful.

"Why did you decide to become a rancher?''

Jeb shrugged. "The corporate world was not for me. I grew up on a ranch, too, and I wanted to get back to that life.''

He studied her, and silence stretched tensely between them. "If you thought I had abandoned Kevin and Cherie, why did you cut all ties to your past and hide your tracks when you moved from Houston to Dallas?"

As she flushed and bit her lip and looked guilty, he wondered if she had been leading him on with an act. How much was she like Cherie? he wondered again.

"I guess deep down there was a part of me that doubted Cherie," Amanda said, so softly that he had to lean forward to hear her, yet leaning closer was a tactical error because he could smell her perfume, see her flawless skin, watch as her tongue slid slowly across her lower lip. His body heat rose and momentarily he lost awareness of anything except a desirable woman sitting inches away. He had to fight the urge to reach out and touch her.

She twisted a string from her cutoffs in her fingers. "I wanted to believe her when she said you didn't care and you had gone, but my cousin has never been a stickler for the truth. She tells things to suit herself. I was scared of just what's happening now. That someday the doorbell would ring and there would be Kevin's father—you—wanting him back." She looked Jeb in the eye. "Maybe I shouldn't have made it difficult for you to find us, but from all indications, you weren't a man I wanted to get to know."

"I suppose not, since I can take him from you."

"I don't think you can," she said coolly, and he realized she was pulling herself together more and more as they talked. "Cherie has gotten mixed up with people in the past that I didn't want to know. Her choice in men would never be mine. Sorry, that doesn't sound complimentary, but Cherie and I are very different.''

"So I'm noticing," he remarked dryly. He wondered if she realized exactly how guilty she looked. But she was different from Cherie. Cherie was a charmer when she wanted something, flirting and using her feminine wiles to sweet-talk someone into doing what she wanted. He had been charmed completely, but marriage had brought reality and another side to Cherie that was far from charming. Cherie would never have been as forthright as Amanda.

Amanda caught another string on her cutoffs and twisted it back and forth between her thumb and forefinger. Otherwise, she looked quiet and composed. He watched her hand, noticing that her fingers were delicate and slender. She did not wear any rings and wore a simple watch with a leather strap circling her wrist.

"I suppose we're going to have to work something out to share him," she said stiffly, and each word sounded wrung from her in agony. "Unless you're still intent on going to court and trying to take him from me completely. If you do that, I'm going to fight you and we'll just end up hurting him."

"I agree."

She let out a long breath and closed her eyes. "Thank you!" she said. "We agree on that much. Kevin should come first."

"If he came first completely one of us would give him up."

She opened her eyes to look at him and he could see the speculation in them. "Maybe not. Maybe he needs a father as well as a mother. But I have to know how you'll be with him. There are things I don't approve of."

Jeb's temper flared and he leaned closer. "Lady, I'm his father. Whether you approve or not, I'll do what I think is best for my son. I won't abuse him, but I suspect I'll let him do things that you and that nanny and the other women in his life would be afraid to let him do. He acts scared of his shadow now."

"He's just shy," she said defensively. She studied him as if trying to figure him out. "Would you strike a child?"

"Never. It shouldn't ever be necessary." Green eyes searched his, and he gazed back steadfastly.

"I hope you're telling me the truth," she said. "Is there any way that you can prove to me that you knew nothing about Cherie's pregnancy? How do I know that you didn't abandon him and now that Cherie has a successful career, you've decided you want your son after all?"

"I can find the person who told me, and you can talk to her. It was Polly McQuarters. She knows I wasn't putting on an act. And what difference would it make to me whether Cherie's career is soaring? You've legally adopted her child."

"She's set money up in a trust for him."

"I don't need or want Cherie's money. I'll bring you records of my income and my net worth."

"You don't have to do that," Amanda said, rubbing her temples.

"I told you about my brothers. There's another family member I haven't mentioned—my mother."

"Kevin's grandmother," Amanda whispered, closing her eyes and experiencing a blow to her middle. A father and now another grandmother. She could feel her child slipping away from her, yet she knew she couldn't fight to shut those two important people out of his life. She opened her eyes to discover Jeb watching her intently.

"I haven't told Mom about her grandson yet. I want you and Kevin to meet her."

"Of course, Kevin should meet her." Amanda laced her fingers together. "It's a shock—to open the door and find Kevin's father and learn he has three uncles and a grandmother. Is there anyone else you haven't told me about?"

"Nope. My father's no longer living. My mother is Lila Stuart and she's raised four boys and she was a damned good mother. She lives in Elvira, a small town near my ranch and Cameron's. She's Elvira's mayor."

"How will I break this to Kevin? He's shy around men. Could you just start coming over and getting to know him and then I tell him?"

"I think it would be better to tell him from the start and then I get to know him. Either way it's a shock, but he's only three. Little kids accept life as it comes."

She caught her lower lip in her small white, teeth. As she gazed into space beyond him, Jeb studied her, thinking she must have been engaged to a real jerk. He thought of Cherie and he could see little resemblance between the cousins. Cherie was a blue-eyed blonde, drop-dead gorgeous, with a lush figure. Her cousin had a more earthy look with her riot of red hair and a smattering of freckles, but, in her own way, she was a beautiful woman. He pulled his train of thoughts away from her and focused on Kevin.

"What have you told Kevin about being adopted?"

"I've told him the truth, but he's only three and I don't think he cares or understands. I always tell him how much I wanted him and how much I love him."

"Can you be more specific about 'the truth'—what did you tell him about me?"

"I told him his mother had to give him up because she moved far away and that she's my cousin. He hasn't seemed to realize that he's never even seen her since the day he was born. I told him that his father was in the army and far away. And I told Kevin I wanted him badly and loved him with all my heart. It's pretty simplified, but he accepts that, and when he gets older and wants to know more, I figured I would explain more. At this point in his life, he doesn't seem to care."

"Sounds good enough," Jeb said, thinking over her answer. "What about Maude—Cherie's mother?"

"Kevin knows Aunt Maude is his grandmother, and she's seen him five or six times, but since she remarried and moved to California, she's out of touch and she doesn't seem deeply interested in him. She's more interested than Cherie is though, because she sends him birthday and Christmas presents and calls him once a year. At the time I adopted him, she went to court with me. Aunt Maude said I'd make a better mother than Cherie."

"I'm sure you do." He thought about the rest of the week. "Would you like to come out to my ranch tomorrow night and bring Kevin? I'll pick you up, take you out there for dinner and bring you home early so he can get to bed."

"Are you that close to the city?"

"It's a long drive—about an hour and a half—but I don't mind. I think we'd better start getting acquainted."

Nodding, she gave him another searching stare. "Are you dating anyone?"

"No, and I don't intend to marry again."

Her eyes widened in surprise and she shook her head. "You look like a man who likes women and vice versa."

"I do like women, but I don't want to get married. Or at least not for a long, long time. Maybe someday, because I'd like more children. I was a fool about Cherie and I don't ever want to go through all that pain again," he said, being completely honest with her because they were going to have to work something out. "Our marriage was wonderful for a time, but then it went really bad." Jeb stood. "I'll leave now and pick you up tomorrow evening. Is half past five too early?" he asked, knowing she got home before that time each day.

"That's fine," she said, standing and walking to the door with him. The top of her head came to his shoulder, and as he looked down at her, conflicting emotions warred in him. He didn't want to find her desirable. He wasn't happy that he wanted to touch her and soothe her and stop hurting her.

"We'll work it out. Kevin is the main consideration, and we'll just have to share him."

"I can do that," she said, but she sounded worried. "I want to know that you'll be good to him. I don't know anything about you except that you married Cherie and fathered Kevin."

"You and I will get to know each other." He hesitated. "Do you have a picture of Kevin I can have?"

"Yes," She left to return in minutes with a picture in a small frame. "I have a lot of pictures. Here's one you can take. I'll look for some more and give them to you tomorrow."

"Thanks."

They both looked at the picture of the smiling child. "He was two when that was taken," she said softly. Jeb noticed that when she talked about Kevin or to him, her tone filled with a special warmth. "He looks very much like you."

"Even I can see a resemblance," Jeb said. "There's no mistaking he's mine," he added grimly, knowing that Cherie hadn't been faithful to him. He glanced at Amanda. "Thanks for the picture."

"I have another copy of it in a scrapbook."

"I'll see you tomorrow evening."

She opened the door and he left, striding down the walk to his car. Jeb drove away, his emotions still churning. Nothing had gone the way he had imagined it would. Why hadn't he stopped to think how attached his son would be to his mother? He supposed hurt and anger got in the way of reason. He was going to have to share Kevin. It could be worse, and Amanda Crockett might be a very nice person. How much was she like her cousin? So far, damn little, or she wouldn't have taken Kevin in the first place.

The boy was too shy. Jeb hoped Kevin would get over his shyness. From the looks of it, he needed a man in his life. Jeb's thoughts shifted to Amanda Crockett and her broken engagement. He could hear the hurt in her voice and he knew why she had taken Kevin. She would fight to keep him because he would be the only child in her life. The ex-fiancé was a real jerk, Jeb thought again.

Amanda Crockett. Jeb thought about the statistics the detective had brought him about her: parents deceased, only child, no family except an aunt, Maude Whitaker, and a cousin, Cherie Webster, twenty-eight years old, an audiologist, no men in her life, attends church each week, a large circle of friends, a broken engagement two years after college. Now he knew more—her perfume, whose scent lingered in his memory, her tenderness with Kevin, her full red lips and long slender legs, and that mass of unruly red hair that had to mean there was a less serious side to her. He had to admit that when they touched or looked into each other's eyes, some fiery chemistry occurred. Sparks flew between them, and he suspected she didn't want to feel any attraction, either, but in those moments, he had seen the change in the depths of her eyes, the sultry intensity. He had felt a tightening in his body, a sheer physical response to nothing more than that exchange of looks.

"Forget it," he growled under his breath, trying to concentrate on the problems ahead.

When Jeb reached his ranch, a full moon spilled silver beams over the sprawling land. Feeling restless, he put the car next to his black pickup in the garage and began to walk, heading toward a pasture where some of his horses were. Two of them raised their heads and came to the fence near him. He stopped to talk to them, wishing he had brought an apple with him.

He moved on, knowing sleep wasn't going to come. How would they divide their time with Kevin? Half a month with one parent, half with the other? Weeks with one, weekends with the other? They would have to go to court, get lawyers involved and get it all settled legally, and he dreaded the entire process. The disruption in Kevin's life wouldn't endear him to a man who had been a complete stranger until half past five this afternoon.

Jeb swore, striding fast, turning and going back to

his house to get his running shoes. He switched on lights in his kitchen, which was big and roomy and had oak cabinets and stainless steel equipment. He thought about her tiny kitchen, remembering the times he had brushed against her. The lady sizzled effortlessly. She had an effect on him that set his pulse racing. *"Think about something else,"* he told himself.

In February he had bought the ranch—including the house, which was only four years old—from a family moving to Arizona, and he had spent little time doing anything to it. He strode down the hall to his big bedroom. He had a king-size bed, a desk and little else.

Pulling on his running shoes he left the house, breaking into a jog. His nerves were ragged, his emotions still churning. Cherie.

What a bitch she had been! Hiding her pregnancy from him and letting him walk out without knowing about his baby. Giving the baby away instantly. Jeb wondered why she hadn't had an abortion, knowing she would have no qualms about it. Maybe she didn't realize she was pregnant until it was too late to get one legally. He was still surprised that had stopped her, but then he remembered Cherie had told him about a good friend in high school who had died from a botched illegal abortion. Maybe fear had deterred her. His thoughts jumped to Kevin.

Tomorrow night he was bringing his son to the ranch! The thought of having Kevin cheered him immeasurably and he began to plan. He would barbecue a chicken and get extra drumsticks since Amanda said that was one of Kevin's favorite foods. He thought of Popcorn, a small, gentle pinto mare. Maybe Kevin would like to ride her.

Jeb yanked off his shirt and tossed it over a bush

beside the road where he could pick it up on his way back to the house. Sweat poured off him as his thoughts danced around the possibilities. This Friday he was riding in the county rodeo. Would Amanda let Kevin come and watch? Jeb suspected that Amanda was going to be less than enthusiastic to learn about his rodeoing.

How would they divide the time? Kevin was so accustomed to being with Amanda, would he resent having to be with Jeb?

Question after question swirled in Jeb's mind as he wondered about the future and went over the past few hours, from the moment he had first looked up and had seen Kevin standing in the doorway, staring sleepily at Amanda.

When his muscles were aching, Jeb jogged back home, knowing he was no closer to answers to his questions than he had been when he started. As he passed the barn and bunkhouse, a tall figure emerged from the shadows.

"Kinda late run, isn't it? How'd it go with your son?"

Jeb slowed and wiped sweat from his forehead with his shirt as he faced Jake Reiner, a fellow saddle bronc rider and horse trainer who was working with some new horses Jeb had bought. Jake was shirtless, wearing jeans, with his shaggy black hair hanging loosely on his shoulders.

"Not like I expected."

"When does anything go like you expect it to?" Jake drawled, lounging against the corral fence.

"I saw Kevin and talked to him a little. He's shy."

"He just doesn't know you. What about his mama?"

"I'm sure she hates me, but she's being cooperative, all things considered."

"Cooperative? When you left here, you sounded as if you would storm her house and bring your son home with you."

"Yeah, I know. I didn't stop to think what I'd do if she and my son were very close and he loved her deeply. Which seems to be the case. And she was told that I abandoned him. My ex-wife was a congenital liar."

"I've seen Cherie. Most men wouldn't care whether she was a congenital liar or a kleptomaniac. She is one beautiful woman. Is her cousin as beautiful?"

"Not in the same way."

"In other words, no." Jake shook his hair away from his face. "So where is your son?"

"I'm bringing them both to the ranch for supper tomorrow night. Want to join us?"

Jake grinned. "No, thank you. I'll leave the family gathering to you. She may look at you as possible marriage material."

"No, she won't. She was hurt by an ex-fiancé, and I think she's as uninterested in marriage as I am."

"If she is, she'd be the first female I've ever known. 'Course, I don't know her yet, but there's no such thing as a woman who doesn't want to marry."

Jeb laughed. "I should have come and talked to you instead of wearing myself down with all my running. Sure you don't want to join us for supper?"

"I'm sure. I'm not much for the domestic scene."

"If you change your mind, come to the house about seven. We should be here by then."

"Sure."

"How's Mercury?" Jake asked, referring to a wild two-year-old sorrel he had acquired.

"He's gentling down. Give me another day."

"Good. You can't sleep, either."

"Naw. Some nights are good, some aren't."

Jeb nodded. "See you," he said, wondering again about Jake's past and what demons plagued him. They had known each other from the rodeo circuit and then they had grown close when they had been together through scrapes in the army. Jake had saved Jeb's life once when Jeb had been shot rescuing an American diplomat who had been taken hostage in Colombia. Yet as close as they had become, there was always a part of Jake shut away from even his best friend. Whatever it was, that dark secret kept Jake on the move.

Jeb turned and jogged to the house, glad Jake was with him, because his friend was one of the best horse trainers in the country. Jake wouldn't put down roots anywhere long enough to really build up his reputation with horses. Jeb knew he couldn't worry about Jake's wanderlust—when Jake was ready to move on, he would move on.

Thinking about Amanda, Jeb showered and sprawled across his big bed, sleep as elusive as ever. Neither one of them was going to like dividing Kevin's time between them.

Jeb stared into the darkness, his thoughts racing over possibilities. What if he talked Amanda into moving to his ranch? With three bedrooms and three baths, there was plenty of room. During the day when she was at work, he would be as good as any nanny. While he worked, he could take Kevin with him, and if he couldn't, he had Mrs. Fletcher, who cooked and cleaned for him four days a week. She was a grand-mother to ten kids, so she would be good to Kevin.

Jeb sat up and rubbed the back of his neck. He slid off the bed and began to pace around the room, switching on a bedside lamp as he thought about the idea of having Amanda Crockett share his house and his life. If they weren't married or dating, they probably wouldn't get in each other's way and they could share Kevin. His ranch house was sprawling and roomy. They would have to share their lives, but maybe they could manage it for Kevin. All week she would be gone during the day. He would be gone all day Saturday.

He shook his head at the thought of a woman underfoot all the time, and he guessed she would take an even less enthusiastic view about having him around. He sat on the edge of the bed and ran his fingers through his hair. Scratch that idea.

Half an hour later the idea came back to him and he mulled it over until the first rays of daylight grayed the night and spilled through the windows. He debated with himself about talking it over with her, but the thought of presenting the idea of them living together at his ranch gave him a queasy stomach. And he could imagine it would take her all of three seconds to kill the notion.

Tuesday evening he was again on Amanda's porch, his nerves jangling as he punched the doorbell. When she opened it and smiled, his pulse jumped. Revealing her even white teeth, her smile held so much warmth, he wanted to reach out and touch her.

"We're ready. Want to come in a moment while I get my purse and Kevin's things?"

"Sure," Jeb answered, and stepped inside. Without the screen door between them, he could get a better look at her. She motioned him toward the living room. "I'll get Kevin."

She wore a blue sundress that left her pale shoulders bare, and with her hair tied in a ponytail, she looked about twenty years old. She didn't have the breathtaking dazzle her blond cousin did, but she was incredibly good-looking.

"Hi, Kevin," Jeb said warmly when the little boy ran into the hall. Instantly Kevin slowed and looked up at Jeb.

"'Lo," he said. Amanda appeared and took his hand.

"I'll lock up, so go ahead and we'll be right out."

Jeb nodded and stepped outside to wait.

Amanda locked the house, switched on the alarm and took Kevin's hand. Dressed in a yellow sunsuit, Kevin clutched his blanket and a small book. As Amanda strolled toward the car, carrying Kevin's car seat, Jeb took it from her, their hands brushing. "I'll buckle this in."

Opening the door, Jeb put the car seat in the back, and Amanda went around to the other side to help.

"These aren't the easiest things to fasten in place," she said. When her hands brushed his again, a current shot through her, and she looked up to meet his gaze.

He was only inches away from her and his dark eyes bore into her. While he studied her, there was no denying that she felt something, yet she didn't believe in chemistry between men and women and she didn't want to feel any magic with this man.

With an effort she looked down at the seat and tried to catch her breath. Jeb had placed a strap in the wrong place and she took it from him, too aware of each contact with his warm fingers. She fastened the strap quickly. "Come on, Kevin."

He climbed into the seat and buckled it while she fastened her own belt and Jeb slid behind the wheel.

"My ranch is southwest of town. It's in the direction of your office."

"You know where I work? Oh, the detective you hired told you. I forgot for a minute. I suppose you know a lot about me."

"A lot of statistics. Where you work, where you go to church, that from all indications you're a good mother now."

"How could a detective decide I'm a good mom?"

"The statistics prove that—you take Kevin places on the weekend, see that he gets to visit his friends, have him on a waiting list for private school, that sort of stuff."

She turned slightly in the seat to look at Jeb. Dressed in a pale blue shirt and tight jeans, he was ruggedly handsome. He didn't seem as intimidating as he had during those first few hours, although he was blatantly masculine. She glanced at his long legs and then shifted her gaze outside.

"Will I see horses?" Kevin asked.

"Yes, you'll see horses, and we have a pond with ducks and baby ducklings," Jeb replied.

Kevin clapped his hands, and Amanda twisted in the seat and saw a sparkle in his dark eyes.

"He's going to have fun," she said solemnly, turning back to look at Jeb again. Was he going to win her son's affections swiftly? With a twinge of guilt, she wondered about jealousy, but she knew that, instead of jealousy, it was more fear that she felt, fear that she might lose Kevin completely. But that was ridiculous. Jeb might be very good for Kevin, but she didn't see how she could ever lose the bond she had with her son. She didn't know what his teen years would hold, but she didn't have to worry about them yet.

Later that evening the same fears and questions rose in her mind as she watched Jeb playing ball with Kevin in his backyard. Laughing, Kevin kicked a big red ball and it rolled along the ground, hit a rock and bounced beneath the rail fence. Jeb's long legs stretched out as he dashed to retrieve the ball. He jumped the fence easily, scooped up the ball and threw it back to Kevin. She watched Jeb leap back over the fence with ease and realized how strong and agile he was—how very male. Kevin needed a man in his life, and Jeb Stuart was going to be good for her son. That thought both tore at her and cheered her. But *she* didn't need a man in her life and she didn't want to find Jeb attractive or appealing or allow him to become an important part of her life.

Later, she perched on a fence and watched Kevin ride Jeb's gentle pinto mare. Next, they went to the pond to see the ducks, then walked back to the house where they had bowls of ice cream. Afterward, they moved to the family room and Kevin got out a coloring book Amanda had brought for him. In seconds he was asleep on the floor.

"It's time for us to go home," Amanda said. "I suppose we should have left when we finished the ice cream, but he was having a good time. You won him over tonight with the horseback ride and the ducks and playing ball with him. He's always loved to play ball."

"He's a great kid, but then I'm prejudiced."

"Yes, he is," she said, looking at Jeb. He was seated in a large leather chair, his booted feet propped on an ottoman in front of him. He appeared as relaxed as Kevin until she looked into his brown eyes. His determined gaze made her heart a skip a beat.

"Kevin is already asleep, so why don't we take this time to talk about what we're going to do. I thought about it all last night."

"So did I," she answered quietly, wondering if he had slept as little as she had. She wished she could put off ever making decisions about how she would share her son with this forceful stranger.

"Good. I'd like to tell him that I'm his father."

"Isn't it a little soon?"

"I don't think so. Kids accept life as it comes to them. I want him to know the truth. Can I come get both of you and bring you here for dinner again tomorrow night and tell him?"

She knew it was useless to tell him that he was rushing her. She gazed into his dark eyes and could see the steely determination, so she merely nodded. A knot burned her throat once again. She wished she could just gather up Kevin and run too far away for Jeb Stuart to find them. He was talking to her and she tried to focus on him.

"Kids adjust to whatever life hands them. You'll see."

She knew he was right, but she was having difficulty adjusting to anything concerning Jeb Stuart. There was, however, no point in postponing the inevitable. She nodded. "Fine."

Jeb stood with an easy grace. "I'll be right back. I have something to show you." He left, and she looked around the large family room that she could almost fit half her house into. The stone fireplace was immense. Bookshelves lined one wall—all empty. He said he had only lived here since February and he hadn't bought much furniture. That was an understatement. He had a large leather sofa and a big matching brown leather chair, two end tables, lamps and nothing else. The plank floor held a shine and everything looked neat and clean, but the room was so bare it looked as if he had moved in yesterday. She thought about her home, which was filled with pictures and books and plants, and wondered if he found it cluttered.

She was already saving money for Kevin's education and she didn't want to use her savings. In any case, she would have to hire a lawyer to help her with the legalities of whatever arrangement they worked out. She rubbed her temples. She had had a dull headache since yesterday when she had opened the door and looked up at Jeb.

Boot heels clicked on the polished floor and then he swept into the room and handed her a folder. "Here are records showing what I'm worth, a sort of résumé that tells as much as I could think of about me, the phone numbers of my brothers. You can talk to them and their wives."

"I suppose we need to know all this about each other," she said reluctantly. She ran her hands over the folder in her lap. "Shall I look at this now or take it home with me?"

"Go ahead and look and then take it with you. The information is yours. I'll put Kevin on a bed."

He picked him up easily, the tender look that came over Jeb's face making her breath catch, and in that moment she knew he would never hurt Kevin. She told herself not to go on hunches or feelings, but Jeb's expression was so filled with love and longing, it was painful to see.

He left the room, holding his son as if he carried fragile china, and her hurt mushroomed. For Kevin's sake, if Jeb were a loving, caring father, she had to share her son's life with him.

Reluctantly, she opened the folder and began to read, surprised by how much Jeb was worth. She thumbed through more pages, seeing the decorations he received while he was in the army. When he returned to the room, she glanced at him and met his shuttered gaze. Returning to her reading, she reached the information about his bronc riding and looked up at him.

"You're a champion saddle bronc rider."

"Yep. That's where some of the money came from, and I've invested it since I was eighteen years old."

"Bronc riding is dangerous, isn't it?"

"So's daily life."

Wondering about him, she lowered the folder and ran her fingers over its smooth cover. "Everyone has secrets. What are your secrets, Jeb?"

"What are yours?" he shot back.

"I've already told you mine. I don't usually tell new acquaintances about my physical limitations, that I can't have children."

"My secrets? My life's pretty open. I have regrets about my marriage. I regret that I was such a sucker for your cousin because that turned out to be one shallow marriage."

Jeb was studying her intently, and she had an uneasy feeling. Intuition suddenly told her that she didn't want to hear what he was going to say next. There was a speculative gleam in his eyes and that look of determination was back in his expression.

"I've been thinking about what we can do, and I have a proposal."

Three

Amanda mentally braced herself. Whatever was on his mind, he didn't look too happy about it himself. "Let's hear your idea."

"I've been trying to think how we can divide up the time." He rested his feet on the floor and propped his elbows on his knees. "Now, hear me out, okay?"

"Sure," she said, her gloomy feelings deepening.

"You said you don't date and you don't expect to marry. I told you I didn't want to marry again for a long time, if ever. I don't like the idea of taking Kevin on weekends, while you have him all week or vice versa or anything like that. If we have to, okay, but I had another idea. Why don't you and Kevin move in here?"

"On your ranch?" Stunned, Amanda stared at him. She almost laughed out loud, except he was so earnest and her son's future was at stake.

"Just listen," Jeb said quietly. "This isn't impossibly far from your work. I have a housekeeper, Mrs. Fletcher, who is a grandmother. She's good with kids and she cooks and cleans for me four days a week. She could be a nanny if I need one, but most days when I work, I could keep Kevin with me. We could share our lives with him so much better."

"I'm sorry, but that's out of the question!"

"Why? You think about it a little. We wouldn't have to divide up the time between us—"

"We can't live here together! I'm sorry, but I'm very old-fashioned about some things."

"We wouldn't be living together in a sexual way. It's like living in the same apartment complex."

"I don't think so," she said, beginning to wonder about his mind. "The world would think we were sleeping together," she said, her nerves jangling at even saying the words. "You know that's what everyone would think."

"Who cares?"

"I care. And I care for Kevin's sake," she said, and Jeb looked startled, as if it hadn't occurred to him that the arrangement might not be the best for Kevin. "I don't want to do that. And suppose you have a date and bring her home for the night. What would you do—introduce me as the mother of your child and a woman who just happens to live here, but oh please, ignore her?"

Suddenly a flicker of amusement danced in his dark eyes and her heart lurched because it made him even more appealing.

"I haven't had a date I wanted to bring home with me in a long time."

"That doesn't mean you won't in the future. I'm

sorry, but it's out of the question, and I think you would have major regrets. You'll fall in love again and marry again. Men like you don't live alone."

The moment the words were out of her mouth she wanted to yank them back, and a flush burned her face. He tilted his head, his dark eyes watching her intently, and something changed in their depths. Her half-dozen words had instantly charged the atmosphere with electricity.

"Men *like me*—now, what do you mean by that?" he drawled, his voice lowering to a husky, sexy level.

She looked away because she didn't want to look into his eyes, which seemed to see too much already. "You're an appealing man," she admitted swiftly, the words almost running together, "and I suspect women are easily attracted to you, in spite of your 'not having a date you wanted to bring home' lately. That will change."

Silence stretched until she was compelled to look around. He was sitting still as a statue, studying her as intently as ever.

"Maybe you and I should try dating."

She did laugh then, and his eyebrows arched. "I don't think so! Neither of us wants that."

"We might fall in love," he said, a sparkle dancing in his eyes.

Now he was flirting, and she experienced a bubble of excitement she hadn't known in a long time. "That's impossible. I don't want to fall in love. You don't want to, either. Besides, if you married again, you'd want another child, wouldn't you?"

The sparkle in his eyes vanished and he stood, crossing the room to her to pull her to her feet. The moment he touched her, tension crackled between them. While his hands rested on her shoulders, he gazed at her solemnly.

"Don't sell yourself short. You adopted one child. You can adopt two."

"Don't give me your sympathy," she snapped, too aware of him and too aware of her racing pulse.

"I'm not, Amanda," he said softly, in a deep voice. He was only inches away and his gaze was locked with hers. Her pulse raced and then her breath caught when his gaze lowered to her mouth. His hands slid slowly down her back.

"Don't complicate our lives," she whispered.

"I'm not. How long since your last date?"

She knew she should move away, but she was rooted to the spot, unable to do anything. Could he hear her thudding heart? Did he know the effect he was having on her? She suspected he knew full well. "Too long to remember," she whispered, an inner voice screaming to move and stop him.

"Same here," he said, although she didn't believe him.

"Don't lie to me, Jeb," she whispered. He leaned down, and she thought she would faint. How could he have this devastating effect on her? Was it because she was so incredibly vulnerable? Was she that lonely and hadn't realized it?

"I'm not lying. I won't lie to you." Watching her intently, he leaned closer.

His lips brushed hers lightly and time stopped. She closed her eyes and inhaled, her lips parting as she swayed. His hands tightened on her waist. *Stop him, stop him* came the voice of wisdom. Was he doing this just to win her over to his way of doing things? Did he have a hidden agenda, or did he just want to kiss her?

His lips moved slowly, so slowly over hers, and she wanted to tighten her arms around his neck and kiss him back, but she knew she shouldn't.

"Oh, don't," she whispered against his mouth.

"Shh, Amanda." He tightened his arms around her, pulling her hard against him, leaning over her to cover her mouth with his. He opened her mouth and his tongue stroked hers and a wave of desire washed through her.

Heat flared in her, desire awakening swiftly. Her hands flew to his arms and she felt his muscles and his smooth skin. He laced his fingers in her hair while his other arm tightened around her waist and he leaned over her, his kiss deepening and driving all thought and caution from her mind. She wound her arms around his neck, feeling the textures and strength of him, smelling soap and aftershave, feeling his heart pound with hers. He was at once danger and desire, awesome strength and sexy confidence. For how many breath-stopping moments did she kiss him back?

Finally, she pushed against him. He released her at once and she gazed up at him. He looked as dazed as she felt, and she attributed their reactions to the fact that neither of them had dated in a long time. He was looking at her as though she were the first woman he had ever seen in his life.

"We shouldn't kiss," she said in little more than a whisper. "Sex will only complicate a situation already too complicated."

"It wasn't sex," he said in a husky voice as his fingers drifted lightly over her shoulder. "It was only a kiss. You and I are both old enough to kiss without the world changing.''

She turned away from him to put some distance between them and to keep him from seeing too much in her expression. It hadn't been only a kiss, she thought. It hadn't been like any kiss she'd ever had before. Instantly she tried to ignore that realization and shifted her thoughts to Kevin. ''We should go home.''

''Don't get your feathers in a ruffle,'' Jeb said easily. ''Sit down and we'll talk.''

''We're not moving in here.''

''All right. What do you suggest? Shall we get our lawyers together and see what they can hammer out?''

''I don't like that idea, either.''

''Nor do I.''

Silence stretched between them, and he waved his hand. ''Sit down and we'll discuss what we can do.''

She sat on the sofa, kicked off her shoes and placed her legs beneath her, too aware that he was watching her every move. ''I don't know what's customary in divorce settlements. I have a friend whose children stay with their father two weekends out of every month.''

''I want to see Kevin more than two weekends.'' Jeb crossed the room and sat on the other end of the sofa, facing her. She drew a deep breath, feeling that he was too close. Her pulse quickened, and she tried to focus on what to do about dividing their time with Kevin.

''I want to see him grow up, teach him things, be with him like tonight.''

''If you and Cherie had stayed married, you wouldn't have seen him often. You would've been away in the army.''

"No, I wouldn't have. I would never have gone into the army if I'd known. I was running away from a failed marriage, from hurt, maybe from myself. Now I'm back home. I know what I want to do with my life, and I want my son."

She had a feeling they were going to end up in court and she hated the thought. "I don't want to fight you over this."

"I don't want you to." He reached over to catch her hand, holding it casually and looking at her fingers as if he had never seen fingers before. "You don't wear much jewelry."

She shrugged, aware of his fingers running lightly over her knuckles, causing tingles.

"I want Kevin to meet my mother as soon as possible. How about all of us going to the rodeo Friday night?"

"You're rushing everything."

"Why postpone life? I want to know my son, and my mother is going to be overjoyed. How about Friday, Amanda?"

"Very well. We'll go to the rodeo with you."

"Good. I'm riding in the saddle bronc event, so I won't be sitting with you part of the time."

"That's all right. I'm sure Kevin will like seeing a rodeo. I've never been to one, either."

"This will be a fun one. I've been thinking about our situation and there's something else I'd like to do. Instead of having a nanny with Kevin next week while you work, let me come get him and bring him out here. I'll pick him up and I'll bring him home. You'll be with him as much as ever, and I'll get to be with him a lot. Surely, you can give me the time with him that you let the nanny have."

Turning cold with concern, she pulled her hand away from his. "I don't know you that well. Give me some time. I don't have a detective to find out everything about you, and I can't just turn Kevin over to a stranger."

"If I take you to court, you'll have to. I'll wait to bring him out here without you, but not too long. He's old enough to tell you if he doesn't like it here."

She bristled at his answer. "You know as well as I do that any adult can frighten a small child enough that he won't tell what the adult does."

"I'm not abusive to small children," Jeb said quietly. "You're scared I'm some kind of monster. Call my brothers, ask them if I can be trusted."

"I don't think that would prove much."

"All right, let me bring the nanny out here. She can hang out with us."

Suddenly Amanda had to laugh at the thought of Caitlin Shore having to follow a cowboy around all day. Then she thought of his sex appeal and knew that Caitlin probably wouldn't mind at all.

"What's funny?"

"Caitlin Shore is my nanny, and I laughed at the thought of her following you around, but then, knowing Caitlin, she'd probably enjoy it because she's sort of man-crazy."

"I will not make a pass at your nanny. No problems there."

"Maybe not for you. I'll think about it." She studied him. "Not all men would be this interested in a child they had known nothing about. I'm surprised you are. You don't look like the type to be wild about a baby."

"He's my son. That's important. Our family was

important to all of us. My dad died when I was nine-teen, but Mom held us all together. There are four boys and we have aunts and uncles and cousins. We are a close family and all of us think family is the mainstay of life.'' He ran his fingers across her knuckles.

"Jeb—"

"There's a law against touching?"

"No law, but I still don't think it's wise. I told you, we have enough complications.''

"A little harmless flirting, a few harmless kisses won't complicate anything,'' he said in that sexy, husky voice that was as soft as melted butter.

"Flirting, kissing, you want me to move in with you. You know it can get terribly complicated. I had a broken engagement and you have a broken marriage. I don't want another heartbreak.''

"Scared of falling in love with me?" he asked softly.

She knew he was teasing because the sparkle was back in his dark eyes, but he was taking them into dangerous waters. "You're flirting again, and I think it is definitely time to go home.''

"Whatever the lady wants,'' he said, standing when she did. "I'll get Kevin,'' he said, and left the room.

She watched him walk away, her gaze drifting down over his broad shoulders and trim hips and long legs. That had been some kiss, and flirting with him was more fun than she'd had in a long time. She shouldn't even think about it. Or about his offer to move to his ranch. Yet she had to think about how they would divide their time with Kevin.

When he returned with Kevin curled in his arms, she knew she was going to have to guard her heart because this man was getting past her defenses in ways that no other man ever had.

If Jeb was this crazy about a son he had never seen until yesterday, he would want more children. For an instant the old feelings of inadequacy taunted her, but she had long practice in dealing with them.

She picked up her purse, gathered Kevin's things and went out with Jeb. She waited in the pickup with her sleeping son while Jeb locked up his house and came back. As she watched him stride toward her, his long legs eating up the ground, she remembered his mouth on hers. What had been his motive in kissing her? He was bound to realize the effect he had on her. Was he just doing it to charm her into getting his own way?

As they drove away, she turned slightly to look at him, seeing the illumination from the dash highlight his prominent cheekbones and throw his cheeks in shadows. "I suppose we've made progress. We got along better tonight than last night."

"What about a month with me and a month with you?"

"No. I couldn't bear a whole month without seeing him and that's too disruptive for him. What happens when he falls and gets hurt or gets sick and wants me to hold him?"

"He may get where he's satisfied to have me around."

"Maybe, but he won't right away."

They were slipping back into the clash of wills, and she couldn't stop it. She'd had fun sometimes tonight, but there was no forgetting that she wanted her son with her and Jeb wanted Kevin with him. No matter how much he had them out to his place and how civil they were to each other, she suspected they were going to end up in court battling, and it depressed her to think of that.

As they drove home, she wondered if Jeb was as tense and worried as she was. Even though he hadn't acted too concerned this evening, she knew he was. And while he seemed trustworthy, she couldn't bring herself to trust him yet with Kevin.

At her house, he carried Kevin to his room. As she watched him go ahead of her, her heart lurched at the care with which he placed Kevin in bed. They looked so right together. He pulled off Kevin's shoes and socks.

"He's all right dressed the way he is. If he stirs, I'll get him into his pajamas," she said.

Jeb brushed a lock of hair away from Kevin's forehead and she turned away, knowing she couldn't be soft or too sympathetic because Kevin's happiness was at stake.

She went to the front door and held it open for Jake. Watching her in that hawklike way he had, he paused in front of her and ran his finger along her jaw. "Don't look so worried. We'll work out something that we can both live with. We both want Kevin to be happy, and I know he needs his mother."

She nodded. Jeb bent and brushed her cheek with a kiss. "Stop worrying," he repeated. "We'll work it out."

Then he was gone, striding away. She hadn't thanked him for the dinner or the evening, yet she couldn't bring herself to call thanks to him. She had a knot in her throat and tears in her eyes. She suspected that she was losing Kevin. Jeb Stuart had enough money and resources to fight a tough court battle. He was the blood father and he had rights.

Amanda swiped at her eyes as she locked up, then, after checking on Kevin, she went to her room. She remembered standing in Jeb's arms, kissing him. She didn't want to remember, but she did in total clarity, her lips tingling. His kiss had been devastating. "Don't fall in love with him," she whispered.

She wondered whether he even remembered their kiss.

Wednesday evening Jeb's nerves were taut even when he played with Kevin after supper. They kicked a ball back and forth, and he was aware that Kevin was more talkative with him. He had hung a child's swing on a limb of a tall elm, and later, he sat and watched Amanda swing Kevin. Tonight she wore a red sundress and sandals and had her hair piled on top of her head. She looked even more appealing than she had last night. He wanted to pull the combs out of her hair, let its silky mass fall over her shoulders and run his fingers through it.

All day long he had looked forward to having Kevin at the ranch again, but he had to admit to himself that he had looked forward to another evening with Amanda. Was she getting to him because he was lonesome? Or because she was part of Kevin's life? Or simply because she was an attractive, sexy woman he found interesting?

He wasn't happy about any of the reasons, but he did like having her around and he liked watching her and he wanted to kiss her again. *Cool it,* he told himself. She was right—they should avoid complications, but last night he hadn't been able to resist kissing her.

He had passed it off to her as nothing spectacular, but that hadn't been the truth. Her kiss had ruined his sleep and was tormenting him now. That and the prospect of telling Kevin the truth. How would the child react? Would he hate Jeb for interfering in his life?

It wasn't until dusk had fallen and Kevin was sprawled on the glider on the porch that Jeb scooped the child up and sat down with him on his lap. As Jeb's insides knotted, he took a deep breath. "Kevin, your mother and I have something to tell you."

Kevin glanced at her and looked at Jeb expectantly.

"Would you like to be alone with Kevin?" Amanda asked, standing and moving toward the back door.

"Stay out here with us. I want you here," Jeb said.

Surprised that he wanted her present, she sat down near them and watched Jeb smooth locks of Kevin's hair back from his forehead. All last night and today she had wondered how Kevin would take the news. Every time father and son were together, she knew this was right and good for Kevin, even if it meant that she was losing him a little. She looked at the two of them together—Kevin in his rumpled T-shirt and faded cutoffs, Jeb in a cotton shirt and jeans. The cowboy and his secret son. She should have known someone would tell Jeb about his baby.

"I love you, Kevin," Jeb said in a husky voice

"I love you, too," Kevin replied politely, and Amanda wondered what he really thought about Jeb.

"Kevin, I've been away in the army and now I'm back home to stay, and I came home to find my little boy."

"You have a little boy?"

"Yes, I do, and I love him very much."

Kevin nodded solemnly, and Amanda could hear the

catch in Jeb's throat and knew he was having trouble controlling his emotions. She laced her fingers together tightly and waited.

"Kevin, I have a surprise for you," Jeb said. His voice cracked and he paused. Amanda saw that his eyes were red, and she felt like an intruder, yet he had asked her to stay.

"I'm your daddy, son, and you're my little boy."

"You're my daddy?" Kevin asked, his eyes widening. When he looked at Amanda, she nodded her head.

"Yes, he's your daddy, Kevin."

Kevin looked at Jeb and then he broke into a smile and Jeb hugged him. When Jeb swiped at his eyes, Amanda stood and walked away, giving them privacy, knowing Jeb would pull himself together swiftly.

"I love you, Kevin," Jeb repeated softly, but Amanda heard him.

"Now I have a mommy and a daddy, don't I?"

A knot burned her throat because she could feel Kevin slipping from her. She tried to reassure herself that she wouldn't lose him and that he would gain from having a loving father.

When she heard Jeb laugh, she knew he was back in control of his emotions, so she returned to her chair, feeling relieved that Kevin had accepted Jeb's announcement so easily.

"Yes, indeed you do. A mommy and daddy to be here always for you."

"Will we all live here together now?" Kevin asked, and Jeb glanced at her before smiling at Kevin. "That's something your mother and I haven't worked out. We're talking about it."

"Are you going to leave again?"

"No. I'm here to stay. I'll always be here for you, Kevin," Jeb said solemnly, and Amanda's heart lurched. This man would forever be part of their lives. What kind of arrangement could they possibly work out that would avoid hurting Kevin?

"Kevin, there's one more thing I want to tell you. I have a family, too, and since you're my little boy they're your family now. My mother is your grandmother. My three brothers are your uncles."

Kevin thought that over for a few quiet minutes. "Am I going to see them?"

"Yes, you will. Particularly your grandmother. She wants to see you badly. Okay?"

"Okay," he repeated solemnly, glancing again at Amanda. Amanda had to admit that Jeb imparted all the facts to Kevin in a quiet, forthright manner the child seemed to accept. He looked pleased to have a daddy. "Are we going to meet tonight?"

"No, but we will Friday night. I'm going to take you to a rodeo and she'll be there. Okay?"

"What's a rodeo?"

"Mostly people riding horses."

Kevin nodded. "Will you read me a story?"

"Sure. Get your book."

Kevin scrambled to get several books they had brought, and the moment the door slapped shut behind him Jeb glanced at Amanda.

"He took it pretty well. He seems happy to learn he has a dad."

"I'm sure he is. Every little kid wants a dad. You were good in breaking the news to him."

"Thanks. He just accepted it with no questions."

"That's because of his age and because you've won him over."

"That's because I love him and he knows it."

They gazed at each other and she knew they both wanted to keep Kevin. Once again she could feel the silent clash of wills, and she couldn't bear to think about giving Kevin up part of the time to this man who was all but a stranger. They sat in an uneasy silence until Kevin dashed back and climbed into Jeb's lap.

Jeb read three little books, and then Amanda stood and announced that it was bedtime even for a summer night in the country.

Jeb drove them home and Kevin was asleep fifteen minutes into the drive. Riding in silence, Amanda looked at moonlight splashing over the sprawling land. Her son's life was changing—Jeb's cowboy influence was going to be strong.

"Penny for your thoughts," Jeb said quietly.

"I'm just thinking about the influence you'll be in Kevin's life. This is all new."

"That doesn't mean it's bad."

She merely nodded and looked out the car window again, feeling hot tears sting her eyes. They would go out again Friday night and Kevin would meet his other grandmother.

"You're worrying."

"Of course I'm worrying. You've turned my life upside down!"

"It hasn't been bad, though, has it?"

"Not altogether," she said stiffly, and lapsed into another stony silence, wishing again she could run away with Kevin but knowing that was impossible.

On Friday night, her pulse began to race as she opened her door and faced Jeb. He was dressed in a deep blue western shirt, jeans and boots and his broad-brimmed black hat. In his hands was a box.

"Come in," she said, stepping back, her heart skipping beats the moment she looked into his eyes. He was handsome, exciting, and she was more on edge than ever because she had mixed feelings about the evening.

Kevin came in and stood shyly in the doorway.

"Hi, Kevin," Jeb said easily, and Kevin smiled at him.

"Hi."

"I brought you a present," Jeb said, handing Kevin the large box.

Kevin took it and looked at Amanda. "Thank you," he answered politely, and Amanda wondered whether Jeb was going to try to bribe his way into Kevin's affections, but then she realized that was unfair because this was his first gift.

"Want to open the box, Kevin, and see what you have?" she asked, knowing Kevin was shy and still not at ease instantly around Jeb.

Kevin nodded and sat down on the floor to take the lid off the box. He pulled out a miniature broad-brimmed black western hat like the one Jeb was wearing, and a grin spread over his face.

"What do you say?" Amanda reminded him.

"Thank you," Kevin said politely, running his small fingers over the hat.

"Put it on," Amanda said, once again having mixed feelings and telling herself it was only a hat and not a new way of life.

Kevin put the hat on his head and smiled at her. He wore black slacks and a blue cotton shirt, and now, with the hat, he looked like a little cowboy.

"Go look in the mirror," she said to him, and he ran off.

"I hope you don't mind, but I thought he'd like to wear it tonight."

"He'll love it."

Jeb nodded and touched her red collar. "You look good in jeans. You look pretty."

"Thank you," she answered, warming, yet feeling that constant caution around him because she didn't know whether he was sincere or merely trying to charm her into accepting him.

"Are you ready to go? Mom checked into the hotel at about five."

"Why didn't she stay with you and ride in with you?"

"She's independent and she likes to do her own thing."

Amanda suspected that Lila Stuart's son had inherited the same traits. "Let me get Kevin and my things."

They drove to a large hotel in downtown Fort Worth and all went inside. Amanda couldn't conjure up an image in her mind of Jeb's mother. He was too tall, too male and forceful. So she was totally unprepared for the woman who came strolling toward them.

Four

Tall, black-haired, with a short, casual hairdo that loosely framed her face, Lila Stuart looked forty years old and had as much commanding presence as her son.

"That's your mother?"

"Yeah. Mom looks younger than she is."

"She looks like your older sister!"

Then she was close, smiling at Jeb, and Amanda was astounded that Mrs. Stuart hadn't remarried after the death of Jeb's father. She was a stunning woman and couldn't fit any grandmotherly image Amanda knew.

"Mom, meet Amanda Crockett. Amanda, this is my mother, Lila Stuart."

"How do you do," Amanda said, trying to not sound cold or angry.

"I can't tell you how much this means to me," Lila Stuart said, taking Amanda's hand. "I hope getting to know Jeb and our side of the family hasn't been too hard on you, but for me it's fantastic to discover I have a grandson,'' she said.

"Kevin, this is my mother and your grandmother, Lila Stuart. Mom, this is Kevin.''

"Kevin, I'm so glad to meet you,'' she said warmly, making no move toward him.

When he stared at Lila Stuart shyly, Amanda prompted, "Say thank you, Kevin.''

"Thank you.''

"Let's go eat and we can talk,'' Jeb said, steering them toward the door.

Amanda soon realized that she was dealing with a woman who knew boys. Lila Stuart ignored Kevin until halfway through dinner, then as they ate, she began to talk quietly to him, and in minutes, he was telling her about his toys.

After eating, Jeb drove them to a sprawling building that held the rodeo. When they walked through the large building both Jeb and his mother constantly saw people they knew and paused to say hello and introduce Kevin and her. She realized that the Stuarts were friendly, outgoing charmers who had a wide circle of acquaintances. They would broaden Kevin's life.

Jeb had seats for them in a box along the front row, and while they had the best view of the arena, Amanda wished they were farther away from the action. The place smelled of sawdust and horses. Entering the box, she held Kevin's hand as she moved to the fourth seat in the row, next to the side of their box. Kevin sat beside her and bounced in his seat with excitement. Lila sat next to him with Jeb at the opposite end. Even with the distance between them, Amanda was constantly aware of him.

While they waited for the rodeo to start, Lila pulled a coloring book and crayons from her purse, and in seconds, Kevin scooted closer to her. Then Jeb stood and lifted Kevin into his seat and hunkered down to talk to Kevin about his coloring while Lila leaned over him, too. In minutes Kevin was happily coloring with Lila commenting on his efforts while Jeb came around and swung his long legs over the row to drop down in Kevin's vacated seat next to Amanda.

"Your mother's a charmer, too," Amanda said without thinking as she watched her son talking to his grandmother.

"*Too?*" Jeb asked, turning to study her.

She faced him. "You know you charm people," she said, amused by his innocent act.

"I didn't know it in this case. I'm glad to hear that you think so," he said, leaning forward with his elbows on his knees, effectively putting his back to his mother and Kevin and enclosing Amanda in a very private space, in spite of being surrounded by people.

"Don't push your luck."

"I'm not pushing anything," he drawled. "I'm sitting here doing nothing."

"You're flirting and getting your way. Look what you've done in a week. Kevin has a father and a grandmother and a whole new family. That's pushing. You've done everything—pushing, flirting, kissing."

"You've done a little of all that yourself."

"Sometimes those things make life more fun," she said in a suggestive voice, unable to resist.

He grinned, revealing even white teeth and looking incredibly appealing. "Aah," he said, "here's a good side to you I haven't seen."

"And the side to me you have seen was bad?" she

asked, teasing him and enjoying the banter and knowing it was like playing with a tiger.

"You don't have a bad side," he drawled, his gaze drifting down to her waist and back up to meet her eyes. "I should have said it's just another intriguing facet to you—one I'm going to explore," he said, his husky voice flowing over her in its own caress. He stroked his finger along her forearm and across her knuckles, and fiery tingles danced over her nerves.

"We'll both have some exploring to do," she said softly, letting her gaze rest on his mouth and wanting him to kiss her again. She was playing with danger and she knew she should stop. Although flirting with him was fun, she suspected that this was not a man to toss idle challenges to. Not unless she wanted him to act on them. Yet, at the moment, they weren't idle; she did want his kiss. She didn't understand her own reactions to him, except that she couldn't remember how long it had been since she had done something reckless, something purely for herself alone.

"Actually, I never dreamed it would be fun to flirt with Kevin's mommy, but it is. You blush easily, you know."

"I know that. And you know which buttons to push to get the reaction you want."

"I hope so," he said, lowering his voice. "It's fun to discover which buttons I get to push and play with," he drawled.

"You can't stop flirting, can you?" she asked, smiling at him, yet feeling her pulse pound with his remarks and the velvety voice that was like a warm caress.

"Not with you. You bring all this out in me."

"And every other female under thirty doesn't? Oh, please!" she exclaimed, laughing softly.

"No, they don't," he said flatly.

"I don't believe that for a minute. Now, behave yourself and put Kevin back in this seat between us. How did we all get moved around like this, anyway?"

Jeb grinned at her. "Around you, I can't behave."

"You're going to be good tonight."

"Now you've given me a challenge."

While she gazed into his dancing eyes, her pulse drummed. How long since she had had anything like this in her life? Since any man had made her feel desirable? "When you and I flirt, I feel as if I'm toying with a tiger."

His brow arched wickedly and his eyes sparkled. "Maybe there's a little excitement in living dangerously."

"My life is quiet and peaceful and I don't need any excitement."

"Uh-huh," he drawled. "I think I want to see how you like excitement. I can't help but wonder just how you'd react. My imagination just runs away with me," he said softly, and she knew he wasn't talking about excitement at all, but about making love. Her pulse skittered and she was giddy from his flirting, yet it was a dangerous pastime for both of them.

"Imagine all you want because that's all you're going to do." Why was she flirting right back with him? Yet she knew why—it was dangerous and it was fun and he was irresistible.

"Another big challenge. Maybe and maybe not. The evening's far from over, and I won't forget," he said, brushing her hand lightly with his fingers. It was the slightest, most casual touch, yet the contact with him was searing, and her breath caught.

She stood and leaned over to look at Kevin's coloring. "That's great, Kevin. Come here and let me see your picture."

Kevin came immediately, proud to show his artwork, and she sat back down, touching the arm of Jeb's chair. "You sit here, Kevin, and Jeb can move over where you were. Then you'll be between your grandmother and me and we can both watch you draw."

Jeb gave her a mocking smile and moved easily. When he stood, his hip was at her eye level, and for an instant, she was intensely aware of his tight jeans and long leg only inches away. Even after he sat down at the end of the row with Kevin and Lila between them, Amanda was still acutely aware of him.

The rodeo started with a parade of men and women mounted on sleek, prancing horses, and Lila Stuart slipped the crayons and coloring book back into her purse as Kevin scooted to Jeb's lap to watch everything.

Jeb sat with them through the calf-roping event and the barrel racing. When he left them, Lila Stuart leaned across the empty seat between them to talk to Amanda.

"I want to thank you for the way you're sharing your baby with us," she said quietly. "I can't tell you how fantastic it is to suddenly learn that I'm a grandmother. I had about given up on my boys, but now—this is truly wonderful and I'm grateful for any time I get with Kevin. He's adorable and I know this has all been hard on you."

"I'll have to admit Jeb's appearance was a shock."

"Jeb can be forceful and very determined to get his

way. It looks as if you're holding your own, though. He's my oldest and has a tendency to take charge because, with three little brothers, he had to take charge at home while they grew up.''

"We're trying to work things out," Amanda said.

"I know you are, and everyone wants what's best for Kevin. If I can ever keep him just for an hour or two while you go out—I would absolutely love it," Lila said, looking at Kevin. "Anytime I can. Just call me."

"Thanks, but I imagine your life is pretty busy as it is."

"Being mayor of Elvira isn't nearly as important as being a grandmother. I'll come if you call. I would love it."

"I'll take you up on that sometime," Amanda said, unable to resist the mother any more than she had resisted the son. Lila Stuart was warm, understanding and trying to cooperate.

Then Amanda's attention shifted to the arena as she heard Jeb's name announced and saw him climb into a chute and slip into the saddle. Breathlessly, Amanda watched, her fingers knotted together as Jeb's horse leaped out of the chute and seemed to land stiff-legged on springs to bounce up again.

Man and horse fought a wild contest, the horse bucking and kicking, Jeb hanging on. At the first buck Jeb's hat flew off. Amanda was torn between wanting to close her eyes and a fascination that kept her gaze glued on him. When the buzzer sounded, he swung his leg across the horse and jumped to the ground, landing like a cat on both feet and striding away while cowboys corralled his horse. Grabbing up his hat, Jeb slapped it against his leg to shake off the dust. Then he combed his fingers through his disheveled hair and set his hat on his head.

As Jeb strode across the arena toward them, her pulse raced. Kevin was clapping and jumping up and down. She hadn't seen him that exuberant in a long time.

More than ever, vitality and strength radiated from the tall cowboy, and desire scalded Amanda as her gaze flicked down his long, lean frame.

Jeb was a new factor in her life, and he was a dangerous one because he flirted and charmed and he could break her heart easily. And was he sincere? Or was he being so appealing to get what he wanted from her—to take Kevin? Was she being taken in by a smooth-talking charmer?

He seemed physically fearless, a daredevil cowboy who wanted her most prized possession, and she knew she had to guard against losing not only Kevin, but her heart.

When the event was over, Jeb was announced the winner.

"Congratulations," Amanda said. "Another win."

"This time. Jake isn't here tonight. When he competes, I have a tougher time."

"Jake is a bronc rider?"

"Yep. That's how we first met when we were teens."

"You have a wild streak, Jeb."

"I'm beginning to suspect that you do, too," he said, touching her hair lightly.

She smiled at him and turned to watch the next event.

They enjoyed the rodeo, but Amanda was too aware of Jeb, who had regained his seat beside her and continued to flirt the rest of the evening. After the rodeo they stopped at an ice cream shop and then he took his mother back to her hotel. Jeb drove Amanda and a sleeping Kevin home, where he carried Kevin to bed.

"Want a glass of tea or a cup of coffee before you go home?"

"I'll take the coffee," he said, tossing his hat on a chair and following her to the kitchen to sit down and watch her while she moved around the room. Aware of his watchful gaze, she put a plate of homemade cookies in front of him and sat down across the table from him while the coffee brewed. Even with a table between them, she was too close to him, too aware of his presence. He looked relaxed, but anytime she met his gaze, a crackling tension snapped between them and it was difficult to look away.

"Mom was in heaven tonight." While he talked, he unbuttoned the top three buttons of his shirt in an idle way. She didn't know if he was even giving any thought to what he was doing, but she was too aware of his muscled tanned chest beneath the open blue shirt, the smattering of dark chest hair. She couldn't keep from glancing at his chest, and the room had grown hotter and she tried to keep her attention focused on his face.

"I don't know whether you have any idea how thrilled she was to learn about Kevin, but I couldn't have made her any happier."

"She told me. She offered to baby-sit anytime," Amanda said, shaking her head. "It's hard to imagine her baby-sitting."

"She meant every word. Call her and you'll see." He leaned forward, narrowing the gap between them, and she drew a swift breath. "Don't worry about the way she would treat him. I can promise you, she'll be good to him.''

Amanda nodded, still wary of leaving Kevin with anyone she didn't know well.

He leaned back. "Mom has wanted a grandbaby probably since Burke went off to college.''

"Now she has one.''

"I had a good time tonight, Amanda," he added quietly.

"So did I, except for watching you ride. You like taking risks, don't you?" She glanced at the coffee, saw that it had brewed and stood to pour them both cups.

"I drink it black," he said as she placed his cup in front of him. "Life is full of risks and some of them make life more interesting. I like challenges and I remember some tonight from you. They were a lot more exciting than that bronc I rode.''

Her pulse was racing and she tried to ignore him and her reaction to him. "Have a cookie. I made them because Kevin likes them.''

She sat down across from Jeb again, and when she glanced at him, he gave her a mocking smile. He leaned forward and took her hand. His thumb ran lightly back and forth across her knuckles, sending tingles through her.

"Jeb—"

"Your pulse is fast, Amanda.''

"This is crazy. We have enough to worry about without flirting with each other. Or are you doing this to soften me up so you'll get your way about Kevin?" she asked, feeling desperate because she liked what he was doing too much.

"Soften you up?" he drawled in a husky whisper,

his gaze drifting down over her. "I expect you're as soft now as any man could hope for."

"Jeb, stop playing with me!"

"I'm not playing with you yet, and when I do, you'll know it. And I hope you won't ask me to stop."

She yanked her hand away. "Jeb," she threatened, and he leaned back, smiling at her.

"What's this school you have Kevin signed up for?"

"Hillcrest? It's a private school. I visited it and had an interview with the principal. It wasn't the only one I went to," she said, going on to tell him about the other schools, yet too aware of him. Her hand still tingled from his touch and his comments echoed in her mind, giving her a bubbling excitement.

He drank his coffee and stood, stretching lazily. "I should go home." He looked at her speculatively as she stood. "I remember your saying something tonight about how I could imagine all I wanted because I wasn't going to get to know your reactions to—excitement." He walked around the table as he talked and her pulse jumped.

"Jeb, I mean it. We don't need to complicate our lives."

"Scared?"

"Scared senseless," she whispered as he reached her and rested his hands on her waist. She should step away. She should do all sorts of things except stand still and gaze up at him and want to walk into his arms.

"We're not—"

"Yes, we are," he interrupted, leaning down to kiss her. He slid his arms around her and pulled her tightly against himself as he leaned over her. Her head spun and her insides turned upside down. She wrapped her arms around him and kissed him as passionately as he kissed her. Their tongues met and stroked and touched, hot, wet and silky, and she was on fire.

When she pushed against him, he raised his head, studying her intently.

She wriggled out of his embrace. "Kisses are fun, but with you, they're a dangerous complication I don't want."

He gazed at her solemnly and nodded, turning to leave the room. She followed and watched while he got his hat and strode to the door.

He turned to her, touching her collar lightly. "Maybe you're right after all," he said quietly. "It was a fun evening, and you've made my mom unbelievably happy. Thanks, Amanda. See you in the morning."

Then he was gone, striding down the walk. "Thanks, Jeb. We had fun, too. It's good for Kevin to have a grandmother."

He waved, looking over his shoulder at her, and she wondered what had changed his mood so swiftly.

She closed the door and leaned against it, remembering his kisses, wondering what was going through his mind now.

As Jeb drove away swiftly, he swore. He was on fire, aching with need, hard, wanting her and too aware that he had complicated everything tonight, but dammit, the woman had been fun to flirt with.

"Keep your distance. Keep it businesslike, Stuart," he told himself, knowing he wasn't going to take his own advice.

All evening long he had been unable to resist her.

And she felt something, too. From the first day, they both had.

He thought about his mother and her joy when he'd broken the news to her about Kevin. Nothing he could possibly have given her would have made her as happy as a grandson.

What were Amanda and he going to do to share Kevin? Over and over the question repeated itself in his mind.

What could they do? How could they divide Kevin's time?

The following Thursday at dawn, Jeb came to a conclusion. He hadn't slept twelve hours total for the past week, and he had to do something. He loathed the idea of a court battle and knew that Amanda did, too.

He drove into town, ran a few errands and called Amanda to ask if he could come over and bring dinner tonight. With a note of reluctance in her voice, she agreed. He knew she wished he would simply vanish out of her life as swiftly as he had come into it, but he wasn't going to.

That night, as he got ready to leave for Amanda's, his stomach churned, and he wondered whether he was making another enormous mistake. But at the thought of Kevin and going to court over visitation rights, he knew he was doing the right thing. Then he remembered kissing Amanda. Her kisses had stunned him because they had stirred him in a way that he couldn't recall happening before, and he felt uneasy again.

Dressed in jeans and a starched white cotton shirt, his excitement building, he drove into town. On Amanda's street he slowed, enjoying the cool spring night, the shady trees and lawn sprinklers swirling, the sounds of kids playing in front yards. He turned into Amanda's drive and stopped the pickup behind her black car.

For the next two hours, his pulse hummed with nervousness as he played with Kevin and chatted with Amanda. His gaze flicked over her casual sleeveless navy blouse and cut-offs, down her shapely legs. As he watched her, his pulse speeded even more because she was a beautiful woman. He had sworn he would never give his heart to another woman and he wasn't ready yet to change. Was Amanda really as warm and loving as she appeared? Or was he being taken in again? His defenses came back up, and the queasy feeling returned to his stomach.

When Amanda had Kevin bathed and dressed for bed, Jeb settled in Kevin's rocker, lifting the boy onto his lap and opening a book. He began to read, aware that Amanda was seated on the foot of Kevin's small bed, watching him as he read to his son. Their son.

Their son. Kevin was hers as much as he was Jeb's. Jeb and Kevin had blood ties, but Amanda and Kevin had heart ties and maybe those went even deeper. As Jeb read, he glanced at her and met her speculative gaze. It seemed to him that they continually sized each other up like two combatants about to go into a fight.

His gaze drifted down over her crossed legs and instantly he jerked his attention back to the book. Kevin's small hand was splayed on a page, and as Jeb read and turned the page, he glanced at Kevin, who lay back in his arms, content to listen to him. A surge of love for his son filled him and he leaned down to kiss the top of Kevin's head, knowing that it would be worth the struggle to work out something that would allow them to share Kevin. Would Amanda feel that way, too? he wondered.

As Jeb read, Amanda listened to his deep voice. How had he moved into their lives so swiftly? She was dazed and wary. Two weeks ago she hadn't known of his existence, and now here he sat with Kevin in his lap while he read to him. And each hour she spent with Jeb, she grew more attracted to him. She had changed clothes three times tonight before she was satisfied with her simple blouse and cutoffs.

She ran her fingers across her brow. The cowboy was a forceful dynamo, getting his way about too many things. He sat in the rocker, one long jeans-clad leg propped on his opposite knee while he rocked Kevin. As she watched them, Jeb leaned down to brush a kiss on the top of Kevin's head.

Too many questions were still unanswered. Would he be as good to Kevin when she wasn't present?

When Jeb finished the story, she tucked Kevin in and kissed him good-night.

"Good night, Kevin," Jeb said softly.

"Night," he answered faintly, and Amanda could hear the drowsiness in Kevin's voice.

Jeb and Amanda walked back to the living room, where he began to turn down lights until only one small one was left.

"What are you doing?" she asked, sitting on the sofa. She was both amused and annoyed that he was taking charge in her house.

"Getting soft lights." He crossed the room to her and pulled her to her feet. "I've been thinking and thinking."

"And I'm sure you came up with another plan," she said, aware of his hands still holding her arms and his dark eyes watching her closely. He hadn't kissed her since the night of the rodeo and his touches had been casual, yet his restraint had made her even more aware of him.

"As a matter of fact, I did," he said solemnly. "I've thought about it all this week. I haven't been hasty or impulsive, and I've weighed the pros and cons."

"Well, now I am curious," she said, wondering what it was and why he was taking such care in telling her.

"You will listen, won't you?"

"Yes, of course." With growing curiosity she waited while he reached into a pocket, pulled out a box and handed it to her. It was a ring box and she stared at it, puzzled. She looked at him questioningly and then looked at the ring box.

"Open it."

She did and a dazzling diamond ring caught the light, sparkling, catching her breath with its glittering possibilities. Shocked, her gaze flew to his. "You're crazy!"

"No, I'm not. I've given this a lot of thought, Amanda. Will you marry me?" he asked.

Five

Stunned, she stared at him, thoughts scrambling in her head. It was impossible. A ridiculous solution. Married to this virile, appealing male, who no doubt would fall in love with someone else in the next few years? It was an absurd solution, a stopgap that wouldn't really solve anything. In spite of the barrage of doubts, her pulse jumped and something inside her wanted to cry out *yes*. How simple it would be to accept his proposal. Marry him and solve so many problems. But create so many new ones.

She remembered that first day when he had sat facing her and told her he wouldn't marry again for a long time—not until he decided he wanted more children. Marriage now would only be a fleeting solution that could vanish like smoke.

"I think marriage would be another complication in our lives."

"One that would be worth the rewards," he said, stroking a tendril of hair away from her cheek. With his warm fingers brushing against her, she tingled and wondered whether he knew the effect he had on her. Was he trying to sweet-talk her into this union? "I know it'll be a marriage of convenience, but that should be all right for both of us."

"Marriage—even one of convenience—is too important to be entered into lightly."

"I agree."

"Then how do you think this can work? You don't even know me."

"I know enough about you, and if you'll consider my proposal, I think you'll see that marriage would be workable."

"I live in the city—you live in the country—"

"I've thought about that. Come here," he said in a husky, coaxing voice. Taking her hand, he led her to the sofa where he sat down and pulled her down beside him, turning to face her. She held the ring box in her lap as she studied him. He was a forceful, appealing man, and she suspected that he was very accustomed to getting his way. *A marriage of convenience?*

Convenient for whom? "I can't move to your ranch."

"Hear me out. As an audiologist, you run your own business. I'll pay you for two days' work so we can live on my ranch. That way you can still work in town by commuting the other three days, or keep your house and live here those three days. It would give you two more days with Kevin than you have now."

"That's rather expensive for you," she said,

shocked that he would go to such lengths to get what he wanted.

"I can afford it and I want to do it. It would be good for Kevin, and I think it would be fair to you. I know I can't ask you to give up your work and I don't want to. I'm just asking you to cut back."

She looked down at the sparkling ring resting against a deep blue velvet lining. A marriage, even in name only, would solve their dilemma. It would give Kevin a father and give her more time with her son. The diamond glittered, a far bigger stone than would have been necessary—no stone was necessary at all— yet in its dazzling depths lay unforeseen pitfalls. She raised her head to meet his gaze, looking at midnight eyes that gave no hint of his thoughts, yet seemed to see everything in her head. She studied him openly, looking at his full lower lip, his well-shaped mouth. His nose was straight and his prominent cheekbones gave a rugged handsomeness to his face. A small, pale scar ran along his jaw. She had no idea how he got the scar and she thought again how much a stranger he still was to her.

"I don't know anything about you. I don't know what causes you to lose your temper and how you would treat Kevin if you were exasperated with him. I don't know what you like, or what you don't like. I don't even know your age."

"Thirty-one."

"I don't know your ambitions. You've given me facts and figures about your income, but I don't even know if those are accurate."

He nodded. "I can give you the name of my ac-countant and my attorney and tell them to answer any questions you ask. I have nothing to hide from you. I'll never knowingly hurt Kevin.''

"You got into a bad marriage the first time. Now you're racing headlong into a second marriage that's loveless. Aren't you making another mistake?''

"I don't think so. This is completely different.''

"What happens when Kevin is grown?''

Jeb reached out to run his finger along her knuckles, brushing them lightly, stirring those tingles that astounded her. She hadn't reacted this way to other men she'd dated. Even with Darren, there hadn't been this powerful physical attraction. What if she fell in love with Jeb?

"We can worry about that a few years down the road.''

She barely heard his answer. This man was sexy, virile, and he wanted more children. He would eventually fall in love and then what would happen? And if she fell in love with him, she would be hurt far more than she had been when her relationship with Darren ended because Kevin would enter the equation.

"What happens when you're married to me and you fall in love with someone else?''

"I won't.''

Annoyed, she tossed her hair away from her face. "You can't know that, and you can't avoid falling in love just because it would be inconvenient. Loving another person isn't a calculated, rational thing. It's an affair of the heart, not the mind.''

"Kevin is the most important person in my life. I won't jeopardize my relationship with him.''

She heard the force in his voice and saw the muscle working in his jaw. She looked at his broad shoulders, the T-shirt clinging tightly around muscled biceps.

One hand still rested on hers; his other hand was splayed on his knee. A hand-tooled leather belt with a silver belt buckle circled his narrow waist. As she pulled her gaze up to meet his again, heat rose in her cheeks.

"What about sex? You don't intend to stay celibate all the rest of your life."

He studied her and the heat enveloping her seemed to burst into flames. Tilting her chin up, he lowered his gaze to her mouth. She couldn't get her breath and her pounding heart was deafening. He was going to kiss her again—she could see it in his eyes. She wanted to stay cool and collected and keep things neutral between them, yet words and thoughts failed her.

"You feel something now, the same as I do," he whispered, leaning closer. Her hands came up to rest on his shoulders and she felt the hard muscles. Then he was too close, his mouth covering hers. Her eyes closed as he pulled her into his embrace. His fingers tangled in her hair and he opened her mouth, his tongue stroking hers while her insides constricted and heated.

Unable to resist, she slipped an arm around his neck, catching the soapy scent of his skin. Her fingers brushed his hair as he tightened his arm and kissed her deeply. Her pulse raced, and a dizzying rush of longing tore at her.

She was lost in kisses that stormed her senses and melted her reserve, and she ignored an inner voice nagging dimly at her. Lifting her into his lap, he leaned over her and cradled her in his arms. Her hand slid down to his solid chest. How could she like kissing him so much?

Struggling to hang on to common sense, she finally

pushed against him and opened her eyes. He paused, raising his head slightly to study her. She wriggled free, sliding off his lap and sitting beside him, overcome with embarrassment and surprise. The ring box had tumbled to the floor. She knew he was watching her. His breathing was as ragged as her own and she had felt his wildly beating heart when her hand had slid down against his chest.

He picked up the box with the ring.

"I'm human," she said. "You've proved I like to kiss." She didn't add that he was the only man she had ever reacted to so intensely and swiftly.

He turned her to face him and she met his gaze. "You're a very desirable woman," he said quietly.

She shook her head. "I can't have a relationship without love."

A shuttered look closed over his features, making her feel as if another barrier had come up between them. "I can't love again, not anytime soon. Your cousin killed that in me. So if that's what you want, I can't give it to you."

"Then we're at a stalemate," she said firmly, watching the muscle in his jaw clench. "I don't want a physical relationship. Sex without love isn't my idea of happiness."

"Fine by me. We'll do what you want."

"You're not going to want to stay celibate." She touched the ring, still nestled in the box that now rested in his hand. "I don't think a marriage of convenience would work."

"Don't say no so fast. Think about it. There doesn't have to be any sex, no intimate relationship if you don't want it." She looked at him, meeting his inscrutable dark gaze. "But there's an attraction between us."

"One that neither one of us wants. Are you ready to fall in love again?"

He looked down at the box in his hand, turning it so the ring reflected the light. "No, I'm not." He faced her and stroked hair away from her face. "I was hurt badly and I don't want to go through that again."

"There you are. I don't, either."

"Well, I still think our marrying is the best thing for Kevin. We're both going to be involved in his life from now on. I say, let's give this a try. We'll leave sex out for now. A marriage on paper and two parents to give Kevin what he needs. We'll share him the simplest way possible. You'd see him far more than you do now."

She couldn't argue that point. It was so tempting, because if she said no, she suspected that Jeb would be a powerful opponent.

He removed the ring from the box and picked up her hand to slide the ring on her finger. Her gaze was trapped by his and she had another dizzying spin, feeling as if she were losing control of her life. "I have to know you better," she blurted.

"Fine. We'll get to know each other, but start making plans and I will, too."

"You're moving too fast."

"I want my son in my life. I've lost three precious years of his young life—his babyhood. I don't want to idly wait now. Will you marry me soon? Think of Kevin, Amanda. I'll be a good dad to him."

She suspected that was the truth, and so far he had been fair with her.

"Marry me," he coaxed in a husky voice that washed over her like a caress.

"Yes," she whispered, wondering if she was destroying a chance for future happiness or heading down a path to lose Kevin. Or would this give them some good years together while Kevin was young and impressionable?

"Yes, I will," she repeated, feeling that she was stepping off a cliff at midnight.

"Great!" Jeb hugged her lightly. "How about lunch tomorrow so we can make some plans?"

She thought about her schedule. "I don't have patients scheduled from noon until half past one."

"Good. I'll pick you up at the office. Think about where you want to get married. We can go to a justice of the peace, a minister, whatever you would like." He stood. "I'll go now and see you tomorrow."

He sounded jubilant—and why shouldn't he? she thought. He had gotten what he wanted. Heading to the door with him, she didn't even hear what he was saying as her thoughts spun and doubts bombarded her.

At the door, he turned her to face him with his hands resting lightly on her shoulders. "Stop worrying. I can practically hear the wheels clicking and I can see worry in your big green eyes. It'll be good, Amanda. I don't ever want to hurt Kevin."

When she nodded, he brushed a kiss on her forehead, his lips warm against her skin. Leaving, he took the steps in one long stride.

She closed the door and leaned against it, holding her hand out before her and looking at the glittering solitaire. "What have I done?" she asked aloud. "You got your way again, Jeb Stuart." She thought about his passionate kisses and her eager response. Was she that love-starved that she had melted and lost her judgment?

Would a marriage of convenience work? Goodness knows, it would be good for Kevin, giving him both a father and a mother. It would save a court battle and dividing time with Kevin between them. And she would have more time with Kevin while he was still preschool age.

On the other hand, it seemed like the most impossible arrangement. Jeb Stuart was a virile male and not one to remain celibate. And she didn't want a relationship without love. Would they fall in love? The thought made her tingle, though it seemed absolutely impossible. She couldn't give him the children he wanted.

She ran her fingers across her brow. Why wasn't there a simple way out of the situation!

She went to her room to spend the next hours restlessly tossing and turning, drifting to sleep near dawn.

At half past eleven on Friday Amanda was in her examining room testing Mrs. Mallory's hearing when her intercom buzzed. "Sorry to interrupt you, but I thought you'd like to know that Mr. Stuart is here. He said he has an appointment with you at twelve for lunch."

"That's right, but it'll be another thirty minutes, Julia, before I'm through here. I'll see him then."

She glanced at the closed door to the reception room and could imagine Jeb in her office, probably pacing the room and looking into every nook and cranny. With an effort she turned back to Mrs. Mallory, who was waiting patiently.

Thirty minutes later when Amanda emerged from her examining room, chatting with her patient, her gaze flitted to Jeb and then back to her patient as she told her goodbye. Then Amanda glanced at him.

"Want to come into my office?"

He rose and followed her into the office. She slipped out of the white cotton coat she was wearing, hung it on a hook, then turned to face him. His gaze flicked over her simple dark blue dress with a straight skirt that looked tailored and prim. Her hair was fastened in a knot on top of her head, but wild, curling tendrils escaped, a reminder of the mass of loose curls that usually cascaded over her shoulders.

"I'll have an hour, and then I need to get back because I see another patient at half past one and I want to get ready for my afternoon patients."

"Sure. You pick the place," he said easily, looking at the diamond on her finger and feeling the same mixture of nervousness and satisfaction. He wanted the marriage and he didn't want it, but it seemed the only solution. The sooner they did it, the more he would like it and that's what he intended to discuss over lunch.

In minutes they were seated in a nearby restaurant on a glassed-in, air-conditioned porch that overlooked the busy street.

While he ate a cheeseburger, she ate a few dainty bites of a Waldorf salad, and he suspected she was as nervous over the coming marriage as he.

"Let's set a date. I brought a calendar."

"This is June. What about the end of July?"

He winced and shook his head. "Let's not put this off. We don't have to plan a honeymoon. Only a wedding ceremony. I was thinking one day next week."

"You're rushing things!"

"No, I just want to be with my son. And I don't see any good reason to put it off. Did you want a big church wedding?"

"Heavens, no! I haven't really thought about our wedding." The moment she said *our wedding,* flutters in her stomach took the last of her appetite. Looking relaxed and self-assured, Jeb sat facing her. Today he wore a long-sleeved navy western shirt, jeans and his black boots. With his black hair and dark clothes, he looked as ruggedly handsome as he looked dangerous.

"Next week," she repeated, her mind reeling at the prospect, yet what good reason could she give for putting it off? Any ceremony they had wouldn't be elaborate or take much planning.

"I made an appointment this morning to talk to your accountant," she said, feeling as if she were prying into a total stranger's business. "I don't want to sell my house right away. For now, I'm not going to do anything with it so I'll have it here if I want to stay in town after work."

"Good idea."

"There are some of my things I'd like to bring when I move to your ranch."

He nodded. "Fine. You've seen my place. There's plenty of room, and as far as I'm concerned, the house is in your charge—do what you want with it, except my office and my bedroom." He grinned, a half smile that was crooked and so appealing it took her breath away. "I assume we'll each have our own bedroom."

"Of course!" she snapped.

"Do what you want." He reached into a hip pocket and produced a tiny notebook and flipped it open.

"Here's a calendar. When and where would you like to get married?"

She still couldn't believe what was happening to her, yet the man waiting for an answer was real and earnest. Dazed, she stared at the month of June.

"I have three or four very close friends I'd like to invite to our wedding. This is as close to a real wedding as I ever expect to come," she said, looking out the window. He reached across the table to take her chin in his hands and turn her to face him.

"You can't tell what the future will bring."

She shrugged. "I don't have any family to attend. I'll call Aunt Maude, but she won't come from California. What about your mother and your brothers?"

"I hope all of them will be there. Mom and Cameron definitely will. Pick a date and I'll let them know."

"Since this is a sham wedding, I suppose a justice of the peace will be fine."

"It's still a legal, binding arrangement, so if you want to marry in your church, that's fine with me."

She looked away, watching traffic flow past on the street outside, but not really seeing any of it while she thought about what she wanted. "Let me call my minister." She looked at the calendar. "I'll ask him if a week from tomorrow is convenient and call you."

"Would you like to call from here? I have a phone."

She nodded and he produced a tiny cellular phone. In minutes she had arranged for a wedding at ten o'clock, the morning of the twenty-third of June. As she handed the phone back, she looked up into his dark eyes. "I haven't had contact with Cherie in three years, but I think we need to let her know."

Anger flashed in his eyes, and his jaw tightened. "I don't owe that woman anything."

"I'll call and tell her."

"Suit yourself. My men and I can move your things to the ranch this week."

She laughed, and his brows arched quizzically.

"That's funny?"

"When you want something, you really go after it, don't you?"

"I suppose I do." He reached out to touch the corner of her mouth, a lazy stroke of his fingers that was tantalizing. "You have a nice smile, Amanda. I hope I can see it often."

"That depends on what you do," she said, unable to resist flirting with him a bit.

His eyebrow arched wickedly this time and a gleam came into his eyes.

"I'll try to think of ways to coax more smiles," he said, his velvety voice lowering another notch. "Maybe getting to know each other is going to be fun after all. Think so?"

"It already is," she answered, throwing caution to the wind.

He drew a deep breath, and his chest expanded, and for the first time, when she looked into his eyes, she could read his thoughts because pinpricks of blazing desire had burst to life in the dark brown depths. While her heart pounded, she was caught and held in his gaze, unable to breathe, unable to look away. Thought processes stopped and her skin prickled with a hungry need while she fought the overwhelming urge to touch him.

"I think I've waded in over my head here," she said breathlessly, barely able to get out the words.

"I won't let you drown." His dark gaze consumed her, and still she couldn't look away. The silence crackled with tension. Watching her with that mesmerizing look, he took her hand, raising it to his mouth to kiss her palm, his warm breath a feather-light touch.

"We were talking about moving," she tried to say with some force in her voice, knowing she was failing. Pulling her hand away from his, she broke eye contact and looked down at her hand in her lap. She could still feel his warm breath on her palm. So light, so devastating.

"I think the subject was my moving to the ranch," she repeated, and looked up to find him still watching her intently, and she suspected that she had subtly changed their relationship, no matter how much she told him she wanted to keep things platonic.

"Come out to the ranch tonight," he said, drawling lazily in a coaxing voice that sounded more like an invitation to bed. "While I cook, you can look the place over again and decide where you want to put your furniture. I really don't care what changes you make, and if you want to buy new furniture, that's all right, too. I'll give you my credit card."

Surprised, she studied him. "How do you know I won't make outrageous purchases that you'll hate?"

"I trust your judgment," he said in a silky voice.

"You're still flirting, Jeb," she accused.

"You started it."

"There's something in you that brings recklessness out in me."

"I can't wait to find out what else I can bring out in you."

"Now, we've got to stop this foolishness."

"Aah, don't. This is getting interesting. Don't stop now."

"Jeb—"

He laughed softly. "I can see the redheaded stubbornness appearing. Do what you want with the ranch. Just don't do the house in pink. I've seen your house and it's attractive. I meant it when I said I trust your judgment."

"Thank you," she said, thinking how polite and flirty they were, yet she didn't want this sham marriage and she was certain he didn't, either. Silence fell between them while she wished there was some alternative.

"For Kevin's sake, we're going to make this work," Jeb said in a deep voice. She met his steely gaze and suspected that if she battled him, she would regret it.

"I need to get back to the office."

Nodding, he rose and came around the table to take her arm. When she was seated in his car, she watched him walk around to get behind the wheel, noticing his snug jeans and trim hips. Realizing how she was studying him and where her imagination was going, she turned her head, but she was acutely aware of him when he got into the car. Why did she find him so appealing? The question taunted her.

Six

Sunday afternoon after church Amanda and Kevin watched while Jeb parked his pickup in her driveway. Another man followed, backing a flatbed truck up the driveway. Both men climbed out.

Kevin was excited, looking forward to the prospect of moving to the ranch, and he raced to Jeb, who swung him up onto his shoulders easily.

A tall, black-haired, broad-shouldered man walked beside Jeb. He was rugged, slightly thicker through the shoulders and chest than Jeb, with powerful muscles. The moment she met his dark-eyed gaze, she knew he was aware of the situation and didn't approve of her.

Kevin laughed, winding his fingers in Jeb's thick hair. "How's my boy?" Jeb asked.

"Fine," Kevin answered, looking happy, and she thought how swiftly father and son had bonded.

"Amanda, this is Jake Reiner. Jake, I've told you about Amanda."

"How do you do," he said politely, and she greeted him politely in return.

"And this is Kevin, Jake. Kevin, this is Jake Reiner." Jake shook hands with Kevin.

"Where shall we begin?" Jeb asked, ending any idle talk. For the next two hours, the men were busy carrying out her furniture. Jeb let Kevin help in tiny ways and put him in the bed of the truck while Amanda helped with lighter belongings. Once, while she stood in the kitchen packing a box, Jeb passed through the room.

"Where's Kevin?"

"Jake's watching him. He's good with women and animals, so he ought to be good with kids."

"This is the superb horse trainer you've told me about?"

"He's the best. You should see him tame a wild horse. The wildest melt for him. So do most women," Jeb added dryly.

"He doesn't approve of me."

Jeb shot her a curious glance and shrugged. "Jake doesn't approve of marriage. I don't think it's personal. He'll never tie himself down to marriage. Hell, he won't tie himself to a job more than a year at a time."

"Why not?"

"I don't know. Besides my brothers, he's my best friend. We're really close, but there are some things I don't know about him. There's something that keeps him from sinking roots anywhere."

"Well, this is one time when I think his dislike is personal. I still don't think he approves of me."

"If he doesn't now, he will. You're irresistible," Jeb said with a sexy leer, and she smiled.

As soon as everything had been loaded, Amanda and Kevin rode to the ranch with the men, and Amanda supervised the unloading of the pickup and truck. It was one in the morning when Jeb drove Amanda and Kevin back to the city.

After carrying a sleeping Kevin to bed Jeb left, hearing the door close behind him.

When he returned to the ranch, he unlocked the back door and entered. He could smell her lingering perfume. Already his life was changing and his house was transformed into unfamiliar surroundings. He walked through the rooms, looking at her furniture. Emotions clashed in him: joy over the prospect of getting his son, worry over a marriage that wasn't a union of love. Were they going to regret this—or would it work out?

On the twenty-third of June, these questions still plagued Jeb as he entered the church. His brother Cameron saw him and came forward to shake his hand. "I wasn't sure you'd show up," Cameron said quietly. "You were supposed to be here thirty minutes ago."

"I didn't want to stand around and wait. Let's find the minister and see if everyone is here. I'd like this wedding to start now. Have you seen my bride?"

"Yep. She's been here almost an hour. Maybe she's anxious."

"I think she's supposed to get here early. Where's Kevin?"

"With Mom. I hope you know what you're doing."

"I do. This will be good for Kevin."

"Jeb, he's three. He'll be grown in fifteen years—fifteen good years of your life. Then what will you do?"

Jeb grinned. "I have fifteen years to figure that one out. Stop worrying. Look at Mom and Kevin. This is the best gift I could have given her."

"That's the truth, but you could have done it without marrying. I think Mom had given up ever having a grandchild, but Stella and I are hoping to give her one."

"I'm sure you will."

Cameron smiled, but the worry didn't leave his eyes. "I hope you'll make it. I still can't believe you're doing this. The wives went off to talk to Amanda. That's one thing—they all seem to like her."

"Good," Jake replied absentmindedly while he glanced at his watch again.

"Here comes Jake. I wish I could get him to come work for me when he leaves you. Then again, maybe this time he won't leave you. Maybe he'll settle."

"When pigs fly."

Jake joined them, shaking hands with Jeb and then with Cameron. "You can't talk your brother out of this?" Jake asked Cameron, who shook his head and grinned.

"You know how mule-stubborn he is."

"The hell with you two."

"I'm going to find the good reverend and get this over with," Jeb said, and walked away. Jake watched him. "I hope he knows what he's doing."

"From what's he told me," Cameron said, "she's as uncertain about this whole marriage deal as he is."

"Am I doing the right thing?" Amanda asked herself for what seemed like the millionth time as she stared in the mirror in the room designated by the church for brides and bridesmaids. When someone knocked on the door, Amanda's thoughts shifted from Cherie. Her best friend, Megan Thorne, entered and smiled radiantly. "How's the bride? Jittery?"

"Of course I'm jittery! There's no way to know whether I'm doing the right thing or not." They had discussed this coming marriage at length, and Megan's cheerful acceptance of Amanda's decision was both a relief and an annoyance. She almost wanted someone to try to talk her out of marrying Jeb.

"You've seen Jeb at his best," Amanda said darkly. "He can be charming when he wants to be."

"He's marvelous, Amanda! I say go for it!"

Amanda nodded and turned to look at herself again. She knew the time for hashing over this marriage decision was past. Within the hour, she would be Mrs. Jeb Stuart.

She studied herself, straightening a lock of hair and feeling so fluttery that she wondered if she really would faint for the first time in her life.

She wore a white silk, knee-length sheath with high-heeled white sandals. Her hair was twisted into a knot on top of her head, tendrils framing her face. In spite of some blush, she thought she looked pale and her freckles stood out more than ever.

"You look beautiful."

"Thanks, Megan." She reached for a bottle of perfume and knocked over a jar of lotion. Taking deep breaths, she set the jar upright.

"Calm down," Megan said cheerfully.

"All my soon-to-be sisters-in-law have been here to see me. I met them last night."

"And...?"

"They're nice and they act happy, but I can see the curiosity in their eyes. I don't see how any of them can approve of this."

"You said his mother does."

"Goodness, yes! She gets her grandson, so she's happy."

A knock at the door interrupted them and Megan opened it, talking to someone briefly and returning with a bouquet in her hands. "This is for you from the groom."

"We weren't going to have any of the trappings. I said I wouldn't have any flowers," Amanda said, taking the fragrant bouquet of cascading white and red roses, white carnations, a few deep purple iris and baby's breath. "It's beautiful!" she exclaimed, inhaling deeply the fragrance of the roses. She looked at herself in the mirror with the bouquet in her hands and thought that, with the flowers, she did look like a bride.

"I think this is going to be a good marriage, Amanda."

Amanda lowered the bouquet and smiled. "Because he sent beautiful flowers? You're an optimist." She glanced at her watch. "I guess it's time to go."

Megan smiled broadly. "Come on, Miss Crockett, soon to be Mrs. Stuart."

With a deep breath Amanda held her bouquet and crossed the room.

As soon as she stepped through the door of the church, entering to one side of the altar, her gaze met Jeb's. He came from a door on the opposite side of the church. He was dressed in a dark suit and tie, and the sight of him took her breath away. He was incred-

ibly handsome. Her pulse drummed, and she was fluttery all over. She knew that with the intense physical
reaction she had to him, she was going to complicate
her life by marrying him.

Megan followed Amanda while Jeb's blond brother
Cameron followed him. Amanda glanced at Kevin sitting in the front row, looking solemnly at her. She
smiled at him and he smiled and waved in return. She
saw him slip his hand into his grandmother's and suddenly she felt better. A grandmother for Kevin was a
blessing.

Her gaze shifted back to Jeb, and she looked into
his unfathomable dark eyes. He looked relaxed, confident, certain of his world. The only thing that be-
trayed his emotions was a muscle flexing in his jaw.
At every step that brought her closer to him, her pulse
seemed to jump a notch until it roared in her ears and
drowned out all other noise. Finally, they stopped and
turned to face the minister.

When Jeb took her hand, his fingers were warm and
strong. She glanced down at his hand and wrist; a
white cuff showed slightly beneath the dark sleeve of
his suit. As he moved his wrist, a gold cuff link
glinted.

Repeating her vows, Amanda felt stiff and cold and
as if she were committing a crime by agreeing to this
sham marriage.

"I now pronounce you husband and wife, Mr. and
Mrs. Jeb Stuart. You may kiss the bride."

She looked up at Jeb, who gazed into her eyes solemnly. Then his gaze trailed to her mouth. He leaned
down to brush a warm kiss across her lips.

After the brief kiss, he took her arm and together
they turned to smile at friends and to go to Kevin. The

simple, bare-bones ceremony was over. There was no
music, no walk back up the aisle together as a married
couple, but Jeb had wanted pictures for Kevin when
he was grown, so there was a photographer taking
shots of everyone. As she turned, her gaze met Jake
Reiner's. He sat staring at her, his dark eyes cold and
grim, and a chill ran down her spine.

"Welcome to the family," Lila Stuart said, and
hugged Amanda lightly, her brown eyes warm and
friendly. She smiled at Amanda and looked down at
Kevin, who slipped his hand into his mother's. She
suspected that he knew something momentous was oc-
curring, even if he didn't understand what it was. Then
the rest of the family swarmed her to hug and wish
her well until the photographer interrupted them.

"Mrs. Stuart, Mr. Stuart, if you're ready, I'll take a
few pictures here and then take some more at the reception."

Mrs. Stuart. How long would it take her to grow
accustomed to being Mrs. Stuart, Amanda wondered
as she turned to face the photographer Jeb had hired.
They posed for pictures, with Kevin in all but one.
Finally Jeb waved his hand, motioning to his family.
"Let's head out for the party," he said easily. "We
can talk there and get more pictures then."

Lila Stuart and Kevin rode with them to the reception. Jeb had rented a restaurant for the next three
hours and it had a glassed-in area overlooking a small
lake. A band played, and for the guests it seemed to
be a festive party. Jeb was charming, and when he
asked her to dance, Amanda moved willingly into his
arms for the first even slightly private moment with
him during the entire day. His arm circled her waist
and his warm hand held hers. They danced to the slow

number and she moved easily with him, looking into his dark eyes and feeling her pulse drum.

"You look beautiful," he said quietly.

"Thank you. You look very handsome."

"Are you doing all right with all of this?"

"So far, yes. But this is easy and you have a very nice family."

"We'll take it a day at a time. I learned the hard way not to plan too much for the future."

"Thank you for the beautiful flowers."

"I thought you should have flowers. We don't know where we're going, Amanda. Maybe we'll fall in love and want memories of this day."

His words rippled over her nerves, and she wanted to believe what he said, but she knew better. This man someday wanted a wife who could give him more children, and she couldn't. She tilted her head to study him. "I thought you didn't want to fall in love again."

"I don't, but as you said, that's something the heart does and not the head. Wisdom and logic don't rule the heart. Besides, we're married, anyway, so why not?"

She smiled and shook her head. "Love isn't ever a convenience."

"Those sound like words of a starry-eyed romantic. You continually surprise me."

"I imagine we're going to continue to surprise each other. We're little more than strangers now."

"We're a lot more than strangers," he said in a soft voice, tightening his arm around her waist. "We don't have to worry about the future now. Today is all we have to face, and enjoying this party with family and friends. And at the moment, I like dancing with you," he said, pulling her closer.

"Aunt Maude called me this morning again to wish me well. She likes you very much."

"She called me, too. She said you're the woman I should have married in the first place."

"Sometimes she doesn't get along with her own daughter."

"I'm sorry she couldn't be here."

"I'm accustomed to being without a family, except now I have Kevin and you and a very big family." She wanted to close her eyes, follow his lead and forget all her worries. And maybe he was right. Take the moment and don't worry about tomorrow. Yet as she gazed into the dark depths of her handsome husband's eyes, she suspected that she should guard against falling in love with him if she didn't want heartbreak.

The party went on until two in the afternoon, and by half past two, everyone had gone except Jeb's relatives, and one by one, they said farewell until only the brothers, their wives and Lila were left. The brothers and their wives were staying at Cameron's ranch until their planes left on Monday morning, so they all drove to Cameron's place. As a result Amanda wasn't alone with Jeb until midnight, when Jeb stood and announced, "I better take my wife and son and go home."

The words made her acutely aware of the awkwardness of their situation. Through the goodbyes and as she watched him carry a sleeping Kevin to the car, her insides grew more fluttery. When they reached his ranch, he carried Kevin toward the house. Following him, carrying Jeb's coat and tie, Amanda watched him be so careful with Kevin. His broad shoulders looked like a bulwark for her son, his long stride easily covering the ground while he seemed to carry Kevin effortlessly.

They moved through the darkened kitchen, and she walked ahead of him to switch on lights.

"Drop my things on a chair, and I'll get them later," Jeb said. Earlier in the evening he had pocketed his cuff links and rolled up his shirt sleeves. His crisp white shirt was unbuttoned to his waist.

They moved into Kevin's room, his familiar furniture now in Jeb's house. "It's not cold. I'll strip him down to his underwear," Jeb said, slipping off Kevin's shoes and socks. She helped, and in minutes, she was leaning over Kevin to kiss him goodnight.

Jeb did the same and they tiptoed out of his room. When they stepped into the hall, Jeb took her hand.

"Let's have a drink," he suggested.

She was tempted to say no, but one look into his dark, coaxing eyes and she nodded. Deep in her heart, she knew she not only wanted to be with him, but after a day with him, dancing with him and constantly being touched by him, she wanted to kiss him.

In the kitchen Jeb opened a chilled bottle of champagne and she watched the pale, golden liquid bubble in the fragile glasses. He carried their drinks outside to his porch where a new monitor was turned on so they could hear Kevin if he woke. Jeb handed her a glass of champagne. As he stood facing her, he raised his glass in a toast. "Here's to our future."

She touched her glass to his, sipped and then raised hers. "Here's to tonight," she said softly, knowing she was once again tempting fate. "For better or for worse, we'll remember this evening forever."

"I think there are some things we've still left undone," he said in a husky voice, taking her drink and setting both glasses on a table.

Seven

Her pulse pounded and an inner voice cried out warnings, but she ignored them. It had been a magical day and night, and she'd had more fun today with Jeb than she'd had in years.

Slipping his arm around her waist, he drew her to him and she came eagerly into his arms. As she looked into his eyes, her pulse leaped. His gaze shifted to her mouth and then he leaned down. His mouth covered hers and desire burst within her, white-hot and all-consuming.

As his tongue stroked hers, he tightened his arm around her. Her hands went to his chest and she pushed away his shirt, which he had long ago unbuttoned, and then her hands were on his bare chest, sliding around to his smooth, muscled back.

Dimly she felt his other hand in her hair and was

aware of pins falling, her hair tumbling over her shoulders.

"Mandy," he whispered, bestowing the first nickname she'd ever had in her life; yet said by him it was instantly special. His gaze held hers. "This is good," he said roughly, and then his arm tightened, holding her pressed against him while his mouth covered hers in a fierce, hungry kiss that turned her to jelly.

Trembling with need, she clung to him, returning his kisses wildly, the fingers of one hand winding in his hair while her other hand moved down his back to his narrow waist, stopping when her fingers touched his belt.

He was warm and strong, all solid muscle. His kisses were hot, heady and demanding. Who was this man who had stormed into her life and swept her into marriage? Kevin's father, now her stranger-husband. Dynamic, sexy, he was a whirlwind, rushing her headlong with him into what? Another heartbreak? Rapture?

He tugged at the zipper of her white silk dress and pushed it off her shoulders. She was only dimly aware of what he was doing because his kisses had shut out reality. His tongue stroked hers, thrust deeply into her mouth, moving in a rhythm that made her think of complete union with him. Her hips pressed against him and she trembled, aching and wanting so much more of him, wanting to touch and kiss him and relish his maleness.

He shifted and his hand pushed her dress to her waist. While he cupped her breast, his thumb caressed her nipple. Moaning with pleasure, she stroked his back, then slid her hand around to his chest as he leaned down, taking her breast in his mouth, his tongue stroking where his hand had been seconds before. Gasping with pleasure, she clung to him.

Jeb shook, trying to hold back, his body raging with desire. He wanted this tall, red-headed woman who was a mystery to him, and who intrigued him. Now she was his wife. Legally married—yet he had agreed to avoid making love. And here he was on their first night, before their vows were twenty-four hours old, breaking that agreement. She was incredibly desirable. Was he making the same mistake again, being swept off his feet by a woman he truly didn't know? Yet in his heart, he couldn't imagine that she wasn't as good as she seemed. Three years of mothering a little boy was a true test of character. And did that make her even more desirable to him?

All day long thoughts had swarmed through his head. When he'd watched her walk into the church, her green eyes wide and solemn, with self-assurance in her walk, his heart had missed a beat. The white silk clung to her slender figure. She had looked elegant, poised and so desirable that he had broken into a sweat and had to turn to look at Kevin and think about his son.

Then through the party, when he had glanced across the room at her or saw her laughing with friends, he wanted to go claim his new wife and take her away where he could be alone with her. When she had stepped into his arms to dance, her green eyes darkening, his desire had compounded. Tension had sizzled between them, racing along his nerves like heat lightning.

Again, when he danced with her, holding her close, he wanted to dance across the room and out the door and take her away with him where he could kiss her.

At last she was in his arms and she was all he had dreamed about and so much more. Trembling, returning his kisses eagerly with her hands sliding over him as hungrily as his moved over her, she was incredible.

Plans, logic, caution were gone. She was a beautiful, desirable woman, and he wanted her. Promises or not, he wasn't stopping until she indicated that she wanted him to.

He inhaled the intoxicating perfume she wore, winding his fingers in her cloud of silky hair. He wanted to strip away her dress and lacy underclothes and carry her to his bed, but he tried to hold back.

Then she pushed against his chest lightly. Reluctantly, curbing his desire, he raised his head and looked down at her. Her green eyes were stormy, her mouth swollen from their kisses and her face flushed with passion.

She reached to pull up her silk dress, but he caught her hands lightly and feasted his gaze on her high, firm breasts, which he had freed from their lacy constraints.

"You're beautiful, Mandy," he whispered, stroking her breast so lightly.

With a gasp, she pulled up her dress, holding it in front of her. "We're going way too fast, Jeb." Her words were breathless and slow, her voice lower and raw with need as her heated gaze ran over his bare chest and he felt as if she had stroked her hands over him.

When she ran her tongue across her lips, he ached to lean forward and catch her tongue lightly with his teeth. Desire burned in her eyes and fueled his own longing.

"A month ago today, I didn't even know you," she continued.

"We're married," he reminded her, wondering why words that usually came so easily failed him now. He wanted her with a driving force that consumed him like a raging fire. His brain couldn't focus on persuasive arguments and he was just trying to hang on to his control. All he knew was that a beautiful, desirable woman stood only inches away, and she had responded eagerly to his touches and kisses and now she wanted him to stop.

"We agreed to keep things platonic, at least for a while. This is too fast for me."

"You liked kissing. Tell me you didn't," he said huskily, running his fingers along her bare arm, over her shoulder and across her nape.

"Yes, you know I like to kiss, but I don't want to get deeply involved in a physical relationship. Not until I know you better." Her voice became even more shaky.

"You feel something every time we touch," he reminded her quietly.

"Yes. I know I can't hide my responses and I don't really want to. At the same time, I don't want to rush too far, too fast and make a terrible mistake that will hurt all of us."

Wriggling with seeming ease, she slipped back into her dress. When she struggled to zip it up, he turned her around. "I'll do that."

"You're making things worse."

"I can't resist," he whispered, leaning forward to brush kisses on her back before he began slowly to draw her zipper up. He heard her intake of breath, and he wanted to unzip her dress instead.

He trailed kisses up, following with the slow tug of the zipper, and then he brushed her hair away to kiss her nape. She turned to face him, taking his upper arms and holding him lightly.

"We have to get to know each other. There are too many things from both our pasts to ignore. We've both been hurt before and don't want to be again. I think the sensible thing to do is to tell you good-night and go to *my* room now," she said, emphasizing the *my*. Swiftly she stood on tiptoe and brushed his cheek with a kiss. "Thanks for so many things today." Then she was gone, hurrying away from him with that sexy walk of hers, and he wanted to go after her and haul her into his arms and kiss away every protest, but common sense said she was right.

Sleep would be impossible and he looked around, wondering if there was anything he could do to wear himself into physical exhaustion and try to forget the only thing he wanted to do. He went down the hall, too aware of passing her closed door, imagining her lying in bed and wondering if she could sleep. He swore under his breath and stopped at Kevin's room to tiptoe inside. The adjoining door to her room was open and he wanted to swear again, thinking how easy it would be to go the few yards to her bed.

Instead he walked to Kevin's small bed and looked at his son sprawled asleep. Smiling, Jeb touched Kevin's hand, brushing his fingers across his son's fingers, and he was thankful she had agreed to the marriage. Now that he had his son, the world was much better. Jeb tiptoed out and went to his room to change to jeans and running shoes. He wondered how long he would have to run to get his raging body to cool down and to get erotic thoughts of Mandy out of his head.

In an hour he returned and took a cold shower. Then he went to the kitchen and poured himself a stiff drink of bourbon and carried it outside to sit on the porch and gaze into the darkness.

What happened if they fell in love? When his marriage to Cherie had ended, he had sworn he wouldn't ever love again, but as time passed and his pain had healed, he had been more realistic about the future, feeling that some day far in the future, he might consider marriage.

Was Mandy right? Were they rushing headlong into disaster? He didn't think so, but he had to admit that they didn't know each other all that well yet. He sighed and stretched out his long legs, remembering totally how it had felt to hold her in his arms, to kiss her and caress her and feel her soft body thrust against his. He swore, knowing he wasn't one degree closer to sleep than he had been before his run. Was she sleeping peacefully? What had those kisses done to her?

Upstairs in her room, Amanda heard the floor creak and glanced at her closed bedroom door. Was Jeb still up? She looked at the clock and sat up in bed, staring at the door and then looking at the open door to Kevin's room, knowing his door to the hall was also open.

How easy it would have been to have yielded to passion tonight. Had she done the right thing? Was it really the smart thing to do? Or should she let go and see where passion took them?

Logic told her she was right in insisting that they slow down and get to know each other before they got into a physical relationship. Yet how difficult it had been to stop kissing him! She had wanted to close her eyes, let go and make love all night long. Instead, she went to the window to gaze outside, amazed that she was living out on a ranch and that Kevin now had a father—amazed that her life had changed completely.

This was the only wedding night she would ever have, and she was spending it alone.

A light knock on her door broke into her thoughts.

Her insides constricted and heat flashed in her while she fought with herself about whether to answer the knock or pretend to be asleep. Even as she told herself to pretend to be asleep, she crossed the room. She was aware of how short her cotton gown was and how scantily she was dressed.

"Jeb?" she said softly, and heard an answer from the other side of the door.

Yanking on a pale turquoise cotton robe, she opened the door to face him. He was bare-chested and barefoot, wearing jeans.

"I can't sleep, either," he said quietly. "Come sit with me outside and have a drink and we'll talk. I promise, only talk."

"I think you gave that promise that once before and didn't keep it."

"You can't fault a guy when the lady is irresistible."

She had to laugh.

"C'mon," he urged. "You can't sleep."

Again there was a quick mental battle between what she knew she should do and what she wanted to do, and what she wanted won. Nodding, she stepped into the hall. He moved away, leaving distance between them.

"At least Kevin can sleep. I've been for a run, showered and had a drink, but I still can't sleep and I wondered if you could. How about a glass of wine or beer or pop or lemonade?"

"I'll take lemonade."

"I looked at Kevin, and he's sleeping peacefully."

"He usually does."

She moved outside and they sat side by side. True to his word, Jeb kept a distance between them, but that didn't stop her acute awareness of him or the longing to reach for him.

"I'd like to teach Kevin to ride if it's all right with you."

"Kevin is only three!"

"He can ride around the corral. I'll watch him."

"Before I know it, you'll be taking him all over the ranch with you."

"Maybe, but I'll take care of him. Let's see how he likes it."

She studied Jeb and knew he was tough and strong. She wondered if he would expect too much of Kevin or take too many risks. So far he had been very careful about Kevin and hadn't done one thing she disapproved of, so she nodded. "All right, if he wants to."

"Stop worrying. You can come with us or come watch. Do you like to ride?"

"Actually, I don't think I've ridden a horse since I was a child and went on pony rides at birthday parties and that sort of thing."

"You're missing something. Mrs. Fletcher will be here to cook in the morning at half past five. Kevin knows her and can stay with her. Come riding with me and let me show you the ranch and we'll watch the sun come up."

"At five-thirty in the morning?" she asked, mildly horrified at the thought of getting up so early. "It's after three in the morning now."

"Then you'll sleep well tomorrow night," he said cheerfully. "Come on."

"I don't know a thing about horses."

"I'll show you. You just need to know the front end from the back end," he said, grinning at her. "Come on. The sunrise will be worth it. That and my company."

She had to laugh at him. "Such modesty!"

"I like it when you laugh," he said softly, reaching over to take her hand and lace his fingers through hers.

"It's usually nice when anyone laughs," she replied lightly, drawing a swift breath when their hands touched. "Tell me about growing up. When did you learn to ride?"

"I don't remember ever not riding," he said easily, and told her about his childhood on the family ranch. All the time they talked, she was aware of her hand in his.

They talked until four and he walked back to her bedroom door with her. "Well, I kept my word and kept my distance. See you in an hour and a half." He turned and sauntered to his room. She watched him until he reached his door and glanced over his shoulder at her. How close they were! And how easy it would be to fly into his arms.

She hurried into her room and closed her door, going to check on Kevin and then crawling into bed and smiling when she thought of some of the funny remarks Jeb had made. Then she drifted off to sleep, remembering dancing in his arms and repeating wedding vows. Mrs. Jeb Stuart.

By six the next morning, she was prickly with awareness of Jeb as she rode beside him, casting sur-

reptitious glances at him and sometimes watching him
openly. He looked totally at ease in the saddle, while
she was as uncertain about the animal beneath her as
she would have been in a spaceship. The horse seemed
huge, but so far she had done nothing more than move
along beside Jeb's black horse. He had given her Popcorn, the same small mare that Kevin rode, which
suited her fine. But after the first few minutes, she
forgot the horse because the man beside her took all
her attention.

They crossed a stream and rode through tall trees
along rolling country and came out on a green pasture
that stretched away before them. When they halted, he
looked at horses grazing peacefully. "I raise quarter
horses. I can show you the papers on their bloodlines.
I have some cattle, but what I love are the horses, and
these are the cutting horses that cowboys use. You'll
have to come watch sometime when I'm working and
you'll see what they can do. You've seen them at the
rodeo."

"Isn't this life harder and far more dangerous than
what you did before when you worked in Houston?"

He gazed into the distance and shook his head.
"Maybe, but I like it a lot better and I'm making a
good living at it." He flicked the reins and moved on.
She followed, catching up to ride beside him. They
were in an early morning dusky light that caught the
silvery drops of dew on the grass and leaves. Morning
doves cooed softly and a hush was on the earth, and
she had to admit that the ranch was beautiful at this
time of day. They reached a swift-running creek, with
clear water splashing over smooth stones and pools of
green water where there were deep holes.

"You have a river on your ranch," she said, looking at the deeper places.

"It's only a big creek and it's great. I don't have to worry about water. I have wells, too."

"Kevin can't come out here. He's little and he can't swim. Last year he was scared of water, but he's gotten over that."

"Don't worry. If I take him out, he'll never be out of my sight."

She looked at Jeb as he urged his horse across a shallow part of the water. She followed, reassured by his promise.

They rode in an easy silence, moving through trees again and climbing a rise to stop beneath a spreading oak. He dismounted swiftly and took her reins. "Come down here," he said quietly, shoving his hat to the back of his head.

Aware of his watchful gaze and her fluttering pulse, she dismounted. His hands closed on her waist and he swung her the rest of the way to the ground. His arm circled her shoulders easily and he turned her to look at the view. Mist hung in the valleys and the first pink rays of the sun shone over the treetops. In the distance she could see the roofs of the house, the outbuildings and the stable, and the silvery ribbon of the creek winding across part of the ranch.

"It's beautiful."

"Very beautiful," he said in a husky voice, turning her to him. And then she was in his arms and it seemed the most natural thing in the world to be there and to be kissing him.

When he raised his head and looked at her, she opened her eyes.

"Someday, Mandy, we'll make love up here beneath this tree and you'll be my woman,'' he said roughly.

''You don't know that,'' she said, more shaken than she had been the night before. ''You don't even know me that well or if you'll like me when you do get to know me.'' His dark eyes blazed and he looked as determined as he had the first day she met him. Even though she told herself that he couldn't know what would happen between them in the future, a thrill of excitement bubbled in her.

''I do know it.'' He lowered his head and his mouth covered hers. He spread his legs and his hand slid down over her bottom, pulling her up against him. She felt his hardness and his iron strength while her pulse roared from his words and his kisses.

She pushed against him, gazing up at him. ''Let's go back.''

He nodded. ''What would it hurt if we fell in love?''

''It wouldn't—if we both fall in love, but if it's only a physical relationship for one of us, then the other one will get hurt.''

''We took some vows.''

''You know what a sham this marriage is.''

''Maybe,'' he said cautiously, watching her. ''But it doesn't have to be.''

''You told me once that someday you want more children. I can't give them to you,'' she said flatly, the old empty feelings of inadequacy rising to haunt her.

He gave a dismissive wave of his hand. ''We can adopt kids. You adopted Kevin and look how much you love him. And he's a good kid.''

''You really wouldn't care if you didn't have any more of your own?''

"No. There are other important ties besides blood ties."

"Some men don't feel that way."

"I'm being truthful with you."

She gazed at the sprawling vista before her, yet was thinking of the past. "For a while I felt so inadequate. Actually, after my breakup with Darren, I felt undesirable. And then I got Kevin and I began to feel complete and a woman again and the physical impairment seemed blown out of proportion."

Jeb turned her to face him. "That's good, because you're one of the most desirable women I've ever known," he said quietly. "I want you, Amanda, and I'm willing to wait until you're ready, but we're already man and wife. It could be good between us."

He kissed her again and this time she let go of her reservations and returned his kisses until they both were half undressed and breathless. She pushed against his chest. "Jeb, I have to be more certain than I am now." She knew it was pointless to add that she wanted more than just to be desired, she wanted his love.

He released her, yanking on his shirt while she turned her back to dress with shaking fingers, too aware of him behind her, of his readiness, his desire.

He helped her mount and then swung easily into his own saddle, his horse prancing slightly before it settled into a walk. She watched Jeb, wondering about him and amazed by what he had said to her in the past hour. *"You're one of the most desirable women I've ever known."* His words strummed over her heart like a melody and warmed her. Yet too much was still left unsaid.

Her gaze ran over him swiftly, over his long legs

and tight jeans and broad shoulders, over the callused hands that could be so incredibly gentle. What did she feel for him? She knew she was falling in love with this tough cowboy. For the first time, she admitted that he had already taken part of her heart. And with every kiss, every hour together, she was more in love with him.

Would it be all right to let go, love him and give freely to him and see where love took her? Her pulse raced at the thought. She wanted to follow her instincts, wanted to let go, wanted him to make love to her mindlessly. *Wait, wait,* argued her logical mind. *Love him and let go,* argued her heart.

For the next two weeks, they lived under the same roof and she tried to adjust to her new life. Jeb seemed to take to it with the greatest of ease, and if he had rough moments, they didn't show.

But she was finding a lot of things a strain. She still worried about Kevin. She was beginning to trust Jeb and she had decided that he would be good to his son, but she knew he was going to let Kevin do things she considered dangerous and teach Kevin things she would worry about. Kevin was already riding in front of Jeb in the saddle when he left the house early in the mornings. And if Jeb didn't ride a horse, he buckled Kevin's car seat into his pickup and the two headed out to feed and check on animals.

She cut her practice back to two days a week, Wednesdays and Thursdays, because she didn't like the long drive into the city, she didn't like being away from Kevin, and, she had to admit, she didn't like being away from Jeb.

She knew she was falling in love with Jeb and had known that for weeks now, but should she let go and give him her heart completely? His words were heady, making her feel desirable, making her long for the real marriage that they were coming closer to each day.

On a Tuesday afternoon in early August, as she stood in the small bedroom they had turned into her office, she saw a pickup come sweeping up to the back door and Jake Reiner jumped out. He was bare-chested and in jeans, his hair wet and slicked back from his face. His long legs ate up the ground as he strode toward the house.

Suddenly alarmed that something had happened to Kevin, Amanda raced to the back door to meet him. Mrs. Fletcher stood at the kitchen sink peeling potatoes.

"Here comes Jake," Amanda said. The moment she swung open the back door, Jake grinned.

"Can you come with me? Kevin and Jeb have a surprise. They want to show you something."

Eight

"**N**ow?" she asked, relief pouring over her and curiosity taking its place. She looked down at her cutoffs, her red T-shirt and her sneakers. "Like this?"

"That's perfect," Jake said, grabbing her hand and heading toward the pickup.

"I'll be back soon," she called to Mrs. Fletcher, and pulled the door shut behind her, laughing and wondering what Kevin and Jeb wanted to show her. Jake dropped her hand and opened the door to his pickup. She slid inside and watched him stride around the front. For the first time she noticed that his jeans were wet.

"You're all wet," she said when he climbed behind the wheel.

He grinned at her again with a flash of white teeth. "Yeah, and it feels good. It's hot enough today to go up in flames just standing still."

"And you're not going to tell me where we're going or what I'm going to see?"

"Nope. They want to surprise you."

"Everything about this ranch is a surprise," she said as they passed the small house where Jake lived. His Harley was parked beneath a shed.

"You like it here, don't you?" Jake asked her.

"Yes, I do and Kevin does. It's been good for him."

"He's a cute kid and coming out of his shell. Sorry, I didn't mean to sound as if something was wrong with him."

"That's all right," she said while the hot wind blew in the open windows against her. She had no idea where Jake was taking her or how he knew where he was going. It looked to her as if they were driving off across open country without following any road, but he and Jeb both seemed to know the ranch as well as she knew her own neighborhood.

"Kevin has never been around men and he was shy when we moved out here."

"He's the first kid I've ever been around. I know horses and bikes, but I don't know kids." He glanced at her. "You've been good for Jeb."

Startled, she looked at Jake, who was staring straight ahead again. "Thanks," she said, wondering when and how she had won the tough cowboy's approval. They hit a bump and she clutched the seat and forgot about Jake, wondering again about Kevin and Jeb.

In minutes they passed a stand of oaks and drove into the open, crossing a pasture to a tall oak where a shiny new stock tank stood in the shade. Jeb's black pickup was parked nearby. The tank was filled with water and Kevin was splashing merrily in it while Jeb sat in the water, leaning back with his arms stretched out on either side of him along the rim of the tank as he watched Kevin play.

Kevin spotted her and started jumping up and down excitedly, and she realized how much he had changed in the short time they had known Jeb. He had lost his quiet manner and was exuberant so much more often now.

She laughed as she stepped out of the pickup and walked over to them. "Is this what you rushed me out here to see? You're in a horse tank! That water can't be clean."

"Sure it is," Jeb said easily, eyeing her. "No horse has been near this tank. It's brand-new—I got it the day before you moved to the ranch. It's got fresh water in it and it's clean enough. Cleaner than the creek."

"Watch me, Mommy. Watch. I can swim!" Kevin exclaimed proudly, and moved to one side of the tank, poised as if he were diving in.

"I'm watching," she said, glancing at Jeb and then back at Kevin, who jumped in and thrashed his way across the tank to the opposite side.

Her heart fluttered because last summer when he was two, he had been frightened of pools. Surprise and joy filled her. Now he could halfway swim and his fear was gone. Enormous relief and pleasure at his happiness with his accomplishment filled her.

"Kevin, that's wonderful!" she cried, clapping her hands.

"Come in," Kevin urged.

"Yeah, come on in," Jeb drawled, and heat flashed in her as she looked at him and met his smoldering gaze. "Scared?" he challenged, and for a moment she forgot everything else as her body tingled.

Kevin splashed to the edge of the tank to look up at her. "Come swim, Mommy."

"Kevin, I don't want to get wet," she said, eyeing the tank and too aware of Jeb.

"Please!" Kevin called, and swept a big wave of water out, splashing her. Squealing, she jumped back and looked at Jeb, who gave her a mocking smile.

Impulsively, she took two quick steps, gave a leap and sailed over the edge and over Kevin, landing on her bottom and splashing water over all of them.

She laughed and came up while Kevin giggled and splashed her.

"Come on, kiddo," Jake said easily, picking up Kevin and swinging him to his shoulders. "Let's you and me go see Mrs. Fletcher about some chocolate ice cream."

Kevin squealed with delight and clutched Jake's hair as they turned toward Jake's pickup.

Amanda started to climb out to go home with Kevin, but Jeb reached beneath the water and took hold of her ankle.

When she turned to look at him, her heart missed a beat. His dark eyes burned with desire. He still had one muscled arm stretched lazily on the rim of the tank, but his other hand was sliding higher on her leg, stroking her below the surface of the water.

She glanced over her shoulder at Jake and Kevin, who were almost to the pickup and talking to each other. Jake buckled Kevin in his pickup and climbed in. Kevin waved, and she waved back.

"Did you tell Jake to take Kevin home so we could be alone?" she asked. Her words were breathless and she was too aware of Jeb, of his bare chest, that sparkled with tiny drops of crystal-clear water over skin that was deeply tanned. He had a smattering of black chest hair that tapered in a thin line toward his navel. She could see he still wore his jeans.

"No, I didn't. That was Jake's own idea. But a damn good one because it leaves you here with me."

"I don't believe you didn't set this up," she said as he closed his hand firmly around her calf and drew her toward him.

"Jake, this is out in the open in full view of anyone who happens by."

"Yeah, so many people pass this way," he drawled, teasing her. He reached out and pulling her to him, and then he kissed her.

She slid her hands over his warm, hard muscles, his chest that was rock solid. His mouth tasted of cool water and then his tongue ignited flames, and she closed her eyes and knew she had to make a choice now.

She wound her arms around his neck and clung to him, cold water rippling around them. How much longer was she going to keep telling him no when she didn't want to refuse him? Why not take some risks? Why not take a chance that he would fall in love with her?

Her heart pounded wildly as she kissed him, and she admitted to herself that she loved this tall, forceful cowboy with all her heart.

As he kissed her, Jeb stood easily, swinging her into his arms, splashing water when he stepped out of the tank.

She was only dimly aware that he carried her through some trees to a secluded grassy spot shaded by thick oaks. He set her on her feet and released her, his dark gaze riveting as he reached out with deliberation and caught the hem of her wet T-shirt and pulled it over her head.

His chest expanded and his appraisal was a warm caress that set her tingling. "You're beautiful," he said in a rough voice.

His hands shook as he unfastened the clasp of her bra, and then he leaned down and took her breast in his mouth, his tongue stroking her nipple.

She closed her eyes, clutching his shoulders, knowing she was ready to take any risk with him. Maybe this was living dangerously, but she wanted to reach out with heart and body and soul to make their marriage work and be a family for Kevin. And maybe win Jeb's love. She was in love with this strong cowboy who had stormed into her life and changed it completely. And she was ready to take some big risks to try to make a real marriage of their paper one.

He might not love her now, but he wanted her, and he seemed to like her. She hoped love would come as naturally as the sun rising. All their futures were at stake and it was a heady choice, but an easy one when it came down to this moment. Night after night she had thought about the attraction between them and where to go with it. To be wise and cautious and wait. Or to go for all she could and hope for the best.

When she tugged at his belt, he raised his head to look at her, questions in his gaze.

"I want you," she said quietly.

His chest expanded and something flickered in the depths of his eyes. "Not ever like I've wanted you," he whispered, pulling her to him to envelope her in his embrace and kiss her hungrily.

She unbuckled his belt and unbuttoned his wet jeans, pushing them away and then peeling down his wet briefs, freeing him.

His shaft was thick and hard and ready and she couldn't get her breath, looking at the perfection of him. He unbuttoned her cutoffs and shoved them away, then removed her lacy underwear. He pulled her down in the grass, leaning over her while he trailed kisses from her throat down across her breasts, stroking her nipple as he kissed her. Then he took her nipple in his mouth to suck and lick and tease.

Moaning softly with pleasure, bombarded by sensations that drove her wild, she trailed her hands over his strong body, discovering him, memorizing every texture, wanting him desperately. She sat up, pushing him down as she took him in her mouth to kiss him.

He groaned, his fingers winding in her thick hair. Then she was all over him, caressing him with her cool, soft fingers, trailing kisses over him. He yanked the ribbon out of her hair and all the fiery locks fell, darker with water, framing her face and curling on her bare, pale shoulders.

Jeb watched her and his heart threatened to pound out of his chest. She was magic and dreams and hot sex. She was all he wanted and had dreamed about since the night he met her. Her body was soft and pink and white. She was beautiful and wildly passionate, coming to him with a hunger that matched his own for her.

Sometime, somewhere she had made her decision about how they would live. This union was the lady's choice. Knowing she wanted him set him on fire even more. Then she lay sprawled across him, one hand playing over his chest, the other holding him while her tongue glided over his hard shaft. He felt he would burst with need and knew he couldn't wait much longer before his control was gone.

He swung her down and moved over her to kiss and stroke her in return while she looked up at him through half-closed green temptress eyes that were filled with desire.

He moved between her legs, his fingers caressing, finding her feminine places and stroking her until she was taut with need, clinging to him. Amanda's hips moved in an age-old rhythm and she shook, wanting him more than anything else.

"Jeb!" she gasped, and then she shuddered and spilled over a brink.

Spreading her legs, he towered over her, male, sexy, ready. And then he slowly lowered himself, the tip of his shaft touching her, setting her aflame all over again, and then gently entering her, filling her.

He went slowly, perspiration covering him, the only indication of the effort it was costing him to slow down and hold back for her.

"Mandy! My Mandy," he gasped, his voice grating and husky while one hand tangled in her hair and the other hand held her.

They moved together and she clung to his broad shoulders, her eyes closed while she was swept into an urgent spiral. Her long legs were wrapped around him and her hands played over his firm buttocks, down to his hard thighs as she pulled him even closer.

They rocked together, Jeb fighting to make it last, knowing he was losing all control. He was aware of her wildly thrashing beneath him while she clung to him tightly. Her hips arched and he could feel her body tense like a spring coiled tighter and tighter.

"Jeb," she whispered, turning her head. Shifting, he kissed her deeply as he thrust into her. She arched against him, her hips moving, and then he was lost, release exploding in him and shaking him, his pounding pulse shutting out all sounds.

Amanda cried out again, clinging to him, bursting with ecstasy as release came, moving with him in a blinding climax.

"Jeb, I love you," she whispered, unable to hold back the words, knowing she had made the fullest commitment possible to him this day. For better or for worse, she had given herself totally to him. Wife, lover, friend—she prayed she could be all three for him and that he would be husband, lover and friend for her.

They moved together, slowing, and then she was caught on another dizzying spiral, clutching him, her hips moving as his slow thrusts and withdrawals were setting her on fire once more.

"Jeb!"

Tension escalated in her, need rebuilding until she burst over another brink and melted into his embrace. He showered her with kisses and stroked her. When she opened her eyes to look up at him, she was shaken, too aware of how much of a commitment she had made, while he may not have made any at all.

Today she wouldn't worry about it. She would take what they had and cherish every moment and memory. She stroked his jaw, feeling the faint stubble, awed by the wonder of him and their union.

"You're beautiful and you're wonderful and you're sexier than I ever thought possible."

"That sounds like a man in the throes of passion."

"Nope. Just an honest cowboy and his awesome lady."

She laughed and picked a blade of grass to trail it over his face and down on his shoulder. "No one has ever called me awesome. You are still foggy from loving."

"*Foggy* isn't the right description," he said, rolling over and taking her with him so that they both lay on their sides facing each other. He brushed her damp hair away from her face. "I'm exhausted and too beat to even stand up."

"You didn't plan all this?"

"Promise. I'm telling the truth. Don't know why Jake decided to take Kevin and go—except Jake is a chocoholic. He loves chocolate ice cream and Mrs. Fletcher has some. Hon, if I was going to plan a seduction, it wouldn't have been in the horse tank."

She laughed and wrapped her arms around his neck, looking at him and wondering if she would ever get enough of touching him or looking at him or talking to him.

"I never would have guessed you'd take that flying leap into the water," he said, grinning at her. She stroked the corner of his mouth, thought about his kisses and pulled his head to her, tugging him closer to trail her tongue over his lips and then to kiss him.

"I intend to keep you guessing, mister," she teased.

"Let me guess how you like this," he drawled. His arms locked around her and he swung her up over him and in minutes she straddled him, sitting up straight to look down at him. His hands cupped her breasts and his thumbs drew lazy circles on her taut nipples while she closed her eyes and gasped with pleasure.

Then his hands slid to her narrow waist and he lifted her up, setting her on his thick rod.

"See what you do to me?" he said in a husky voice.

Hunger for him shook her and she slid slowly down on him, feeling him enter her again, and then they were moving, lost in another wild union that shut out the world.

He stroked her breast while his other hand went between her thighs, to stroke and touch her. She gasped with pleasure, intoxicated with desire and fulfillment and the knowledge that Jeb wanted her and wanted to give her pleasure.

They moved together until she cried out and fell across him, sprawling over his broad chest and thrilled to feel his strong arms wrapped around her.

"I don't want to ever go home," she whispered. "This is paradise."

"I don't want to go home for days because I want to keep making love to you all the rest of this day and night. And I'll want the same thing tomorrow." He rolled her over again and propped his head on his elbow while he stroked her hair away from her face. "Move into my bedroom with me."

"You're sure?"

"Yes."

She thought about all the move would mean and knew it was what she wanted, too. Her heart thudded with joy at his request and she nodded. "Yes, I will."

"Aah, Mandy. This is good. So damned good."

She wrapped her arms around him and pulled him closer. "I think so, too."

For the next half hour they lay in each other's arms and talked and then Jeb stood and carried her back to the tank, stepped into the water and lowered her into it with him.

His body was sleek and warm in the cold water and in minutes she could feel the change in him and knew he wanted to love again.

"Jeb, we're in the water."

"Yeah," he said, covering her mouth with his and stopping any conversation. He kissed her hard and long and she forgot any protests and in minutes he pulled her over him. She straddled him again and slid down on him, moving with him for another plunge into rapture.

This time when she sat beside him, she caught his hand as he started to caress her.

"We should go home."

"Why? Mrs. Fletcher will take care of Kevin. We have privacy and who do you need to see or talk to?"

"I guess no one if Kevin is all right."

"You know he is."

"You get your way again."

"I hope so, lady." He stood and picked her up again. "Come here."

He carried her easily to his pickup, opened a door and leaned down. "Get that blanket," he said.

She grabbed a light cotton blanket in multicolored stripes. When she covered herself with it, he grinned. "That isn't why I picked that up. If I had you to myself, I'd lock us in the house and throw all your clothes away."

"Thank goodness this is one time you can't and won't get your way! And you're making me blush again."

"That's no reason to blush. I'll give you a real reason to in a minute."

"Forget it, cowboy. Let your imagination cool down."

"It can't when I'm with you."

Her heart raced because she was having the most fun she'd ever had in her life. He was virile, sexy, exciting. His hair was dry now and locks fell on his forehead. He was confident and caring at the same time and she never wanted the day to end. She didn't have even the tiniest regret. Everything felt right and good and promising for a future together.

They reached the place where they had made love before and he set her on her feet, taking the blanket from her and spreading it on the grass.

"You can't tell me you didn't plan this," she said, watching his muscles ripple in his arms and back as he worked.

"I swear I didn't," he said. He straightened up, his grin fading as he looked at her standing nude before him, and she didn't care because she wanted to look at him and touch him and kiss him.

"Mandy," he whispered, drawing her to him and fitting her into his embrace, leaning down to kiss her hungrily as if it were the first time all over again.

They spent the late afternoon beneath the trees, making love leisurely, talking, touching, and she was in paradise.

"Jeb, we have to go home. I'll be so embarrassed."

"Shucks, honey, we're married! There's nothing wrong with a husband and wife disappearing for a few hours."

"I think it's more than a few hours, and Mrs. Fletcher will want to go home."

"I can remedy that. I'll call home." He was up and

striding away before she could answer. She watched him walk easily away, nude, confident, so sexy.

He was back in a few minutes. She felt ridiculous, lying on the blanket totally naked, and had flipped it over herself. He came striding back dressed in his jeans and carrying his phone, his watch and her T-shirt.

"These are dry. Your other clothes are back there. I called home and Mrs. Fletcher can stay with Kevin for another couple of hours and I told her we'd be home then."

"Jeb! That's downright decadent."

"I didn't tell her what we've been doing," he said, grinning at her. "I just said I was delayed and you were with me and could she stay longer. She didn't mind, so that's that. And I asked her if she could stay Saturday night. I want to take you dancing, although what I want most is just to be in bed with you."

His words thrilled her and she was excited by the prospect of going dancing with him. He stretched out beside her, unbuttoned his jeans and turned to take her into his arms. "Get this out of here," he said, tossing the blanket off her.

She saw that he wore nothing under his jeans and that he was aroused and ready for her again. She went into his arms eagerly, wanting him with an unending need that shocked her.

It was dusk when they dressed and he kissed her long and hard before climbing into his pickup to return to the house.

While Amanda talked to Kevin, Jeb talked to Mrs. Fletcher and then joined them. They spent the next hour with Kevin and put him to bed at nine.

As they tiptoed out of his room, Amanda took Jeb's

hand. "We haven't had any dinner yet. Mrs. Fletcher left a lot of food. There's some cold chicken and—"

Jeb picked her up and turned down the hall. "I'll tell you what I want—the wedding night we never had. Food can wait, lady. This is more important."

Her heart thudded and she wound her fingers in his hair to cling to him.

"You're a sex-starved, lusty cowboy."

"And you, ma'am, are the hottest wench around. What you do to me is magic and I can't wait," he whispered, closing his door and setting her on her feet.

Amanda gazed into his dark eyes and could hear only the pounding of her pulse. His gaze lowered to her mouth and her breath caught as he leaned forward. He wrapped his arms around her and kissed her, pulling her up against him. In seconds they were shedding clothes and moving to the bed together, all thoughts of dinner forgotten, as they made love again, consumed by wild passion.

At two in the morning as she lay in his arms in his big bed, he stroked her shoulder lightly. "I hear rumbles that I think are coming from my stomach. I didn't have lunch or dinner. That fruit and biscuit I had yesterday morning was the last food I've eaten."

"Are you complaining?" she asked in a sexy, languid voice, rising up on an elbow to look at him.

"Hardly," he answered, stroking her bare breasts and nibbling on her throat. "This is a lot better than cold chicken."

She laughed and rolled away from him. "Come on, cowboy. I'll feed you."

"And then we're coming right back to bed."

"Maybe," she said, slanting him a saucy look over her shoulder. "You'll have to entice me."

"I'll remember that, and it's a promise."

She scooped up her T-shirt and dropped it over her head. It came only to her thighs, but she knew they would have the house to themselves because Kevin would sleep soundly for hours longer.

She watched as Jeb pulled on his jeans and buttoned them, then came to drape his arm across her shoulders.

They ate cold chicken and a tossed green salad, and she heated steamed carrots. After dinner Jeb got a beer and poured iced tea for her, and they sat and talked at the kitchen table for another thirty minutes.

Jeb propped one foot on another kitchen chair and sipped the cold beer, feeling it go down his throat while he watched her. He knew she was wearing nothing except her provocative T-shirt and the thought was driving him wild. He marveled at himself; he had made love to her all afternoon and evening. He should be satisfied, and able to get his thoughts back to the ranch and everyday things. Instead, all he could think about was her body and how easy it would be to slip the red T-shirt over her head and how much he wanted to do so.

She was unbelievably passionate, something he had suspected she would be, but her eagerness still amazed him. All he had to do was start to think about this afternoon and he would become aroused again.

Would they have a real marriage after all? The thought cheered him. He wanted a family like the one he had known.

Right now, all he wanted to do was to go around the table, take her into his arms and pull off that red T-shirt.

Amanda was telling him something, but he wasn't hearing a word of what she was saying.

"Jeb, are you listening to me?"

"Sure, honey. Well, actually, I'm remembering this afternoon and thinking what I'd like to be doing right now."

She tilted her head to study him while he got up and left to turn on some music. He came back to take her hand and pull her into his arms to dance with her. She smiled up at him. "I don't do my best dancing when I'm barefoot."

"I think it's the best. I like it best when you're only wearing that sexy shirt that clings to you. Or no shirt at all."

"I'm not dancing naked."

As he chuckled, he pulled her closer and they slow-danced and she could feel his arousal. Desire was burning again in her. Then the song ended and a fast number came on and they danced together, Jeb turning her, his hand drifting lightly across her bare bottom when he got the chance.

The moment his fingers stroked across her bottom, her insides tightened and she wanted him as desperately as any time earlier. She locked both hands behind his neck and swiveled her hips against him and he groaned, pulling her tightly into his embrace. In minutes he carried her to bed and they made love long into the night, falling asleep a few hours before dawn.

"Jeb," she said sleepily in the first rays of morning light.

He stretched and then kissed her. "Yeah?"

"Kevin won't know where to find me."

"You can tell him today that you've moved in with me. He'll accept it and that will be that."

"I suppose you're right."

It was almost seven before Amanda was showered

and dressed and in the kitchen, ready to fix breakfast for all of them and expecting Kevin at any moment.

Jeb came striding into the room and kissed her, taking cups of coffee from her and setting them on the table.

"Kevin likes swimming so much, we might think about a pool in a year or two."

"That's a lot of work and expense."

"We can talk about it. It would be good for him."

"Are we arguing already?"

"Never."

Giddy with happiness, she laughed and Jeb grinned at her. She knew they were both on a high from love and she hoped it would last.

During the next weeks, into late August, Amanda was in paradise with Kevin and Jeb. The tall, tough cowboy came home early and played with Kevin, and as soon as Kevin was in bed each night, Jeb pulled her onto his lap or carried her to bed to make love.

One Monday afternoon Amanda heard a car coming up the road. She watched out the front window, wondering who was coming and thinking it must be someone for Jeb. To her surprise, it was a taxi.

"Who would come out here in a cab?" she asked herself aloud as she stared at the cab, unable to imagine who was in it. Jeb's mother always drove when she came.

It slowed and stopped and Amanda watched the driver get out and remove three large suitcases, but still no passenger had gotten out of the taxi.

Curious, Amanda went to the front door and swung it open to watch the driver hold the back door of the taxi. A long shapely leg appeared and then a woman stepped out. She wore skin-tight hot pink capri pants and a sleeveless, tight-fitting hot pink top. Her golden hair was almost white and framed her face in a mass of loose waves. As she started toward the house, Amanda stared in shock. Why would Cherie come to the ranch for a visit?

Nine

"**I** know I should have had my secretary call," Cherie purred, smiling broadly at Amanda as she approached her. She walked up and hugged her lightly, perfume assailing Amanda, and then she stepped back, smiling confidently.

Amanda stared at her, feeling the same deep shock as she had last June when she had opened the door to face Jeb.

"This is a surprise. And it'll be a surprise for Kevin, Cherie," Amanda said, worried about Kevin and how it would be for him to meet Cherie.

"May I come in?"

"Yes," Amanda answered carefully, still worrying about Kevin and what this was going to mean to him. At the moment he was away with Jeb, and she was glad he wasn't home. She needed time to discover what was behind Cherie's sudden appearance. And she was certain there was a purpose in Cherie's visit.

"Kevin isn't here right now, but since he's never seen you, this will be an adjustment for him."

Cherie smiled and looked around the room. "What a nice, homey place you've made this," she said, but her voice didn't sound convincing.

Amanda motioned to a chair and watched her cousin as she sat down. Show business had changed her, and she had a poise she hadn't had before. Her looks were even more spectacular with her big blue eyes and her lush figure. Diamonds adorned her fingers and wrist. Amanda became uncomfortably aware of her own appearance. Her red hair was up in a ponytail with locks that had fallen free around her face. She was dressed in a blue T-shirt and cutoffs and wore no makeup. She felt frowsy and plain next to Cherie, who sat with her legs crossed.

"Jeb isn't home?"

"No. And he's taken Kevin with him."

"Out riding the range with the cows and horses. How's your arrangement working?"

"Our marriage is fine," Amanda said uneasily.

Cherie laughed. "You don't need to pretend with me. Remember, you told me that you and Jeb did this to give Kevin a home." Her smile vanished and she leaned forward, suddenly looking solemn. "Amanda, I realize I've made some terrible mistakes."

A chill ran down Amanda's spine. She could guess what kind of mistakes Cherie had decided she'd made, but she wondered what was motivating her. Cherie couldn't have suddenly developed love and longing for a child she hadn't seen since the day he was born— a child she had been more than happy to give away.

"Jeb was a good husband. I've been married to two real jerks and my last marriage is over. I'm divorced and wiser, and I realize that I threw away the best man I've ever known."

Amanda's chill turned to ice because she knew that Cherie could charm any man if she set her mind to it. And Jeb was not only human, he had been married to Cherie and once upon a time was in love with her.

"We're married," she said softly.

"I can't imagine it really means much to either one of you. You yourself told me when you married him that it was for Kevin's sake. I know this is inconvenient—"

"Inconvenient? Cherie, we're a family."

"Not as much a family as Jeb and Kevin and I," Cherie said softly. "Amanda, I'm Kevin's blood mother. I was the wife Jeb was wildly in love with. Is he wildly in love with you?"

Amanda stared at Cherie, hurt and fear and anger springing to life in her.

"It might have just been for Kevin when we married," Amanda said stiffly, "but it's more than that now," she finished, the words having a hollow ring. She didn't know for certain the depth of Jeb's feelings for her. And she was too aware that he had never said he loved her. Not even in the throes of passion had the words crossed his lips.

She stared at her cousin and wondered if her paper marriage was going to crumble right here and be over before it had really started. "People fall in love fast sometimes, Cherie. I think you have yourself before," Amanda gently reminded her. To Amanda's horror, Cherie's eyes filled with tears that spilled over and she pulled a handkerchief from a purse and dabbed at the tears.

"I was wrong and did the wrong thing. I gave away my baby and tossed my husband aside. I shouldn't have done either."

"Cherie, I legally adopted Kevin. I'm his mother."

"I'm his real mother and Jeb and I can give him a real family."

Feeling numb, Amanda heard noise at the back of the house and, with a sinking feeling, realized that Jeb and Kevin were home. Once again, she wanted to wrap Kevin in her arms and protect him. She knew her cousin far too well to imagine that Cherie was suddenly struck with a longing for her child.

"Excuse me, Cherie, but I think I should tell Jeb we have company."

"Not company, Amanda. I'm family."

Amanda left the room, hurrying to the kitchen, hearing Jeb and Kevin laughing over something.

She stepped inside the room and Jeb glanced at her as he pulled his dusty shirt off. "Whoa—I'm hot, dirty and headed for a shower, and Kevin is, too." He frowned and became still, his voice changing. "What's wrong, Amanda?"

"Jeb, we have a visi—"

"Jeb!" came Cherie's voice as she brushed past Amanda, sweeping into the room and crossing to Jeb to stand on tiptoe and kiss him on the mouth, wrapping her arms around his neck. Extricating himself, he stepped back and frowned.

"Cherie?"

"Kevin, this is Miss Webster," Amanda said to Kevin, who was staring wide-eyed at Cherie.

"Don't be so formal, Amanda. Kevin. Little Kevin," she purred softly. "I'm your real mother."

"Cherie," Jeb said in a deadly quiet voice, sweeping Kevin into his arms and moving past Cherie to hand him to Amanda. "Want to start a bath for Kevin?"

"Yes," she said, looking into dark eyes that held all the rage she had seen that first day she met him. Kevin continued to stare openmouthed at Cherie. Amanda carried him out and heard Jeb moving around the kitchen.

Kevin looked up at her. "You're my real mommy," he said in a troubled voice.

"Yes, I am," Amanda said with certainty, feeling sure Cherie was up to no good. "Cherie is my cousin, Kevin, and she's the woman who gave birth to you, but you're my little boy and I'm your mother and Jeb is your daddy and we love you with all our hearts."

He hugged her and she knew she would be covered with dust, but she didn't care. She wondered what was happening in the kitchen.

Jeb yanked his dusty shirt back on and got himself a beer, turning to face Cherie. "What the hell is going on?"

She pouted and studied him. "That's not much of a greeting."

"Cherie, why are you here?"

"Jeb, don't be so harsh! I know I deserve it, but I made a dreadful mistake." Her eyes filled with tears, but Jeb's patience was short. She had caused him a lifetime of grief in the short time he had known her and he knew now how deceptive she could really be.

He had been charmed and burned once, he wasn't going to let it happen twice.

She dabbed at the tears. "When we divorced, I lost the best man I've ever known."

"Oh, please," Jeb said in disgust. "You can pack up and head back to wherever you live."

"Jeb, I'm sorry. I'm divorced and I've finally realized what I had with you," she said.

Jeb stared at her. "It's over, Cherie. I'm married to Amanda. I'm a very married man."

"You both did that for Kevin. She told me that herself. I know you as well as I know Amanda. You didn't come home and fall in love with her. You married her to give Kevin a father and mother. Tell me that isn't true," she accused, batting her eyes at him and moving closer. "Jeb, remember the fun times we had—"

"All I can remember are the bad times. They canceled out the fun times." Too well, he remembered how charmed he had been by her and how full of fun she had been when he met her. Now all he could see was the woman who had given away their son and never told him about her pregnancy.

"You can't be in love with Amanda. I know you and I know her. She's not your type."

"I do love her," he said firmly, realizing that he had never admitted it to himself, not even with all their lovemaking. Was he really in love with his wife? He had been so busy with getting to know her and living with her, he hadn't stopped to think about it. She was all he admired and found desirable in a woman. He didn't hear what Cherie was saying to him, as he gazed out the window and thought about making love to Mandy.

"Jeb?"

"Sorry, I was thinking about my wife, Cherie."

"Don't shut me out, Jeb," she said softly. "Give us another chance," she said.

"Not in the next six lifetimes," he said. "We're through, Cherie. I'm trying to forget."

She cried softly, and he noticed that she managed to cry without smudging her makeup, but he supposed it was something she'd learned to do. "But you're going to let me get to know my son, aren't you? Surely his blood mother has that right. I can go to court, you know."

"Don't threaten me," he said in a quiet voice.

"And don't hold my son from me," she snapped. "I can go to court and it will give me tons of publicity."

"Bad publicity for abandoning your baby, not telling the father you're pregnant and giving up your baby."

"There's no such thing as bad publicity. Do you know how much publicity a custody battle would get me?"

"Dammit, Cherie, don't you drag my—"

"Our son! Jeb, he's very much mine, too. Don't worry. I'm not going to court over him. I just want to see you both again." Her voice changed to warm honey and she moved close to Jeb to draw her fingers along his jaw.

"Will you let me get to know Kevin? That seems like something small to ask. I know I made terrible mistakes, Jeb. Don't make me keep suffering for them."

He wondered how much she meant what she said. She had lied to him so many times during their marriage that he found it hard to trust her, yet there was a chance that she was telling the truth. And he knew she could go to court and cause a lot of trouble for them because she was Kevin's natural mother.

"All right, but don't hurt him."

"I wouldn't think of it."

"Oh, yes, you would. What do you think you just did when you came bounding in and said, 'Kevin, I'm your real mother'?"

"Maybe I handled that poorly, but I was carried away. He's my baby, and I don't even know him."

"And that was your choice."

"You've gotten tough, Jeb. The army must have changed you."

"It wasn't the army, Cherie."

"You must still feel something for me or you wouldn't be so bitter."

"Cherie, I promise you, the only woman in my life is Amanda. I lo—"

Cherie placed her fingers on his mouth. "Don't say it. You're just saying things because you're angry, and I know I deserve your anger. But don't tell me what a wonderful marriage you two have. I know it was for Kevin."

"It's getting to be a good marriage," he said evenly. Cherie was a beautiful woman, fantastic to look at, yet facing her now, all he felt was a dull anger. Even the anger and bitterness had begun to fade. It was a relief to know he was over her.

"Can I stay and talk to Kevin a little?"

As he stared at her, wanting to refuse, she touched his chest.

"Please, just for a little while. Don't refuse me get-

ting to know my child," Cherie said in a small, help-
less voice.

He remembered how badly he had wanted to see
Kevin and get to know him, so reluctantly, he nodded,
knowing she was Kevin's mother and it was only right
that she could see her son.

"Yes, but be careful. Don't disrupt his life."

"You're angry with me," she said, pouting. "I'm
sorry, Jeb. I can't ever tell you enough how sorry I
am. I know now what kind of man I was married to
and I wish I could undo all my mistakes."

"The past is over and forgotten, Cherie. There's a
bar in the family room and you can get a drink. I'm
going to shower."

She ran her hand along his arm. "I haven't forgotten what muscles you have," she said softly, looking
up at him. "I haven't forgotten anything."

"Well, I have, and what I didn't forget, I'm trying
to forget." He moved past her and left, her perfume
lingering in the air. He had felt nothing when she had
touched him. He wanted her out of his house, but he
knew he had to let her see her son. He strode down
the hall, going to Kevin's bathroom.

Amanda was bathing him and he was laughing with
her over something. She looked pale, and spots of
color were high in her cheeks. Otherwise, she didn't
look as if anything unusual had happened, but the moment her green eyes met his gaze, he could see the
worry in them.

"Can he splash a minute?"

"Sure," she said, standing. "Now that he can swim,
I don't worry as much about him."

"He's all right. You don't have a teacup of water
in the tub, and we're right here and can hear him play-

ing,'' he said as they stepped into Kevin's bedroom. Jeb placed his hands on her shoulders. "Cherie asked to stay and get to know Kevin a little. I can't deny her that."

Amanda looked at the open bathroom door and frowned. "I suppose we can't, but it's hard to believe she really cares about him."

"I agree, but there's a chance she's being truthful. And she reminded me that she can take us to court."

"Oh, Jeb!"

"I don't think it would do her any good, but it won't hurt to let her get to know him a little, so I told her she can stay."

Amanda had a sinking feeling, looking up into Jeb's gaze, which was as unreadable as ever. Was it as simple as he was saying—or had Cherie rekindled some spark in him? Cherie was a gorgeous woman with a fabulous career. What man wouldn't be charmed by her? Amanda nodded and turned back to get Kevin out of the tub.

"I'll get Kevin dressed," she said stiffly, wondering how much Cherie was going to disrupt their lives and how much she was going to try to win Jeb back.

Had he asked her to stay here at the house? Then Amanda remembered the taxi. Cherie couldn't get one to come back out here after six o'clock. Amanda glanced at her watch. Cherie would never get one later this evening.

Anger filled her. They would have to ask Cherie to stay or Jeb would have to drive her back to town to her hotel.

Grimly, Amanda helped Kevin dress. "Sweetie, Miss Webster wants to see you, so she'll be here with us for a little while."

"I'm hungry."

"We're going to eat as soon as you and your father get cleaned up enough to sit at the table," Amanda said, helping him dry and dress, while her thoughts were on Cherie and the evening ahead of them.

As they went to join the others, Amanda felt that her world had been invaded by a foreign presence. Cherie didn't belong in their home with them. She knew her cousin too well. Cherie had a nice side, but she was accustomed to getting her way and could get ugly when thwarted.

Cherie sat in the family room, looking poised for a camera, glancing up when Kevin and Amanda entered the room.

"None of us has had supper yet, Cherie. Would you like to join us?" Amanda reluctantly offered.

"Yes, I'd love that. Jeb asked me to stay," she said slyly. "I hope it isn't inconvenient."

"I hope not, too, Cherie. I'll get supper if you'll excuse us."

Cherie looked at Amanda with smug amusement. "Sorry, Amanda, but I am part of their lives. A very important part. Jeb and I had some wonderful times together."

"I'm sure you did," Amanda said quietly, and turned to go to the kitchen, anger shaking her.

Jeb had asked Cherie to stay. How would he be able to resist the woman? A star—gorgeous, sexy, charming when she wanted to be—how long would it take before he succumbed?

Dinner was quiet except for Cherie. Kevin had withdrawn into a shell, as quiet as he had been before moving to the ranch. Cherie had brought toys that fascinated him, including a toy fire engine and a model airplane that had a remote control. As soon as they finished eating, he began to play with his new gifts.

At half past eight Amanda put Kevin to bed. When she returned to the family room, she heard Cherie's peal of laughter and entered to see Jeb smiling and Cherie still chuckling. Amanda knew she was right, Jeb would never be able to resist Cherie for long.

"I suppose I should call a taxi now if you'll tell me where the phone is."

"You'll never get a cab out here, Cherie," Jeb said dryly. "I can take you back to town or you can spend the night."

"Whatever you prefer," she said, catching her lower lip in her teeth and looking directly at Jeb, ignoring Amanda. It was an hour-and-a-half drive into Dallas, and depending on Cherie's hotel, it could be even farther. It would take three hours for Jeb to come and go.

"Just stay. It'll be easier," Jeb said, glancing at Amanda, who looked away. She didn't want him to take Cherie home, but neither did she want Cherie moving in with them. "Someone can take you into town tomorrow," Jeb added. "I'll get your things," he said, standing and walking out of the room.

Cherie looked at Amanda and smiled. "You can't lose him," she said softly, "because you never really had him."

"Don't push it, Cherie. If you want to see Kevin, all right."

Cherie's brows arched. "This is a side to you I haven't seen, little cousin. You're in love with him, aren't you?" She laughed. "Small wonder. I'll get Jeb to show me where I sleep *tonight*." She put an emphasis on the word *tonight* and smiled again at

Amanda, who felt another flash of anger. Cherie was so confident where men were concerned, and small wonder. How many times in her life had a man not done what she wanted? There were three divorces, but in each of those, she suspected that Cherie had decided it was time for the divorce before the man had. Even with Jeb.

She heard them talking in the hall. It was twenty minutes before they returned, Cherie laughing again and Jeb smiling at something she had said.

They sat down and Amanda found it difficult to enjoy any light conversation while Cherie constantly flirted with Jeb and talked about her success as a singer. "I've signed for a movie deal," she announced smugly.

"Congratulations," Amanda said.

"That's great," Jeb said quietly. "What is it and who's producing it?"

They listened while Cherie talked about the movie plans and Amanda wondered what she really wanted. Why did she want Jeb back now? She still didn't think Cherie wanted Kevin, and with a movie deal, there was no way Cherie would want to live on the ranch. She studied her cousin, curiosity nagging at her.

The evening seemed interminable until Cherie announced she was turning in and left with smiles for Jeb.

As soon as she had gone, Jeb stood. "I'm getting a beer. Let's sit outside awhile. The air's thick in here. Want something to drink?"

"I'll come help. I'd like iced tea."

As soon as they had their drinks they walked out on the porch, where it was dark and cool and quiet. Crickets chirped and in the distance she could hear the deep croak of a bullfrog, but she couldn't enjoy the lovely night. She was too aware of the sexy woman asleep down the hall, a woman who wanted her husband and her child, a woman who was an intrusion in their lives.

They sat in silence, each lost in their own thoughts, and Amanda wondered whether Jeb was withdrawing from her. What was running through his mind? She had heard him laugh with Cherie, and she had listened to Cherie's outrageous flirting. Amanda touched her cold glass to her throbbing temple and prayed that Cherie wouldn't be with them long.

"She asked me if she can stay longer to get to know Kevin."

"Longer?" Amanda's dread deepened.

"I can understand how she feels about him. I know how I felt. I can't deny her getting to know her own son, Amanda. Neither can you. She's his natural mother, and that has to count for something."

"I'm the one who loves him and cares for him and sits up at night with him."

"I know she gave him away. Everything she did was wrong, but she's asked to stay a few days just to get to know him. I can't deny her that and neither can you. I don't want her here any more than you do."

"Don't you?" Amanda couldn't keep from asking.

"No, I don't," he said in a level voice, setting down his half-empty beer and reaching for her hand. "Come sit in my lap."

She went willingly and he pulled her to him to kiss her.

After a moment Amanda straightened to look at him. Black locks of hair fell across his forehead and she pushed them away. "She wants you back."

"I don't want her," he said firmly. He framed Amanda's face with his hands, looking at her for a long moment before he leaned forward to kiss her. His mouth opened hers, his tongue stroking hers, and then he wrapped his arms around her tightly and leaned over her, cradling her against his shoulder while he kissed her.

She returned his kisses, too aware of her throbbing head, the miserable day, Cherie in the house with them and Cherie wanting Jeb. A woman totally accustomed to getting her way with men wouldn't be one to give up easily. Then Jeb shifted, holding her tightly against him while he kissed her deeply and she forgot everything, clinging to him, wanting him with a huge ache in her heart.

In minutes he stood, holding her in his arms and carrying her down the hall to their bedroom. As he set her on her feet, he closed the door behind him. "She's at the other end of the hall."

"Then why do I feel her presence in here with us?" Amanda asked.

"Forget her. I can. And I'll bet I can see to it that you do."

"Oh, Jeb. All I can think is that she wants you back and no man has ever been able to resist her."

He ran his hands through Amanda's hair, framing her face. "I don't want her back, Mandy. Not now or ever."

She gazed up at him in the moonlit room and wondered if he could resist the seductive wiles of Cherie.

"I told you I can make you forget. Let's see how long it takes," he said in a husky voice, kissing her and pulling her into his embrace. She leaned away and shook her head.

"Jeb, my head is throbbing."

"I can cure that, too," he whispered, his tongue flicking in her ear, and then his warm breath was on her throat while he caressed her nape and trailed kisses to the corner of her mouth, his tongue sliding over her lower lip.

She inhaled swiftly, trying to catch her breath, desire blossoming in her. His tongue stroked hers and his hands moved over her, sliding up her rib cage, cupping her breasts. He pushed away her blouse and unfastened the clasp on her bra while he kissed her and then his thumbs lazily circled her taut nipples.

She moaned softly, moving closer against him while she wrapped her arms around his neck and kissed him with all the pent-up longing and love she had.

He leaned against the wall and spread his legs, cupping her bottom and pulling her up against his hard arousal.

She ached with wanting him, loving him. She fumbled with his buttons and belt, pushing away his shirt and then shoving down his jeans.

He peeled away her cutoffs and silk panties and lifted her into his arms while he kissed her hungrily. "Put your legs around me," he whispered, and nibbled at her neck.

She held him tightly as he slid into her, filling her, his heat melting her. They moved together, lost in sensation, and she clung to him, wanting to give to him, wanting to take from him, knowing that, at this moment in time, they were one and all was safe and well.

Ecstasy burst in her and she clung to him, hearing him say her name as he thrust wildly with his release. He slowed and held her tightly, kissing her throat, car-

rying her to their shower, where he set her on her feet
and turned on the water.

After a quick shower they toweled dry and in
minutes were in bed, loving again as he trailed kisses
slowly over every inch of her. "I want to love you all
night, to show you just a little of what I feel for you,"
he whispered. She trembled with love and joy at his
words and tender kisses and slow caresses.

She clung to him tightly, loving him, wanting to
hold him forever. "I love you, Jeb," she whispered,
meaning every word, not certain about him. And then
thoughts shattered and the world was mindless, sensations bombarding her, an insatiable need for him
driving her to a frenzy until her release burst and she
felt his shuddering release.

He held her tightly, showering her with kisses and
rolling over to hold her close.

Exhaustion enveloped her and she lay locked in his
arms, stroking his smooth back, sliding her hand over
his firm buttocks, down to his muscled thigh.

Jeb fell asleep locked in her arms without another
word about Cherie. Amanda lay staring into the darkness, Jeb's dark head on her shoulder while he slept.
She stroked his hair and wondered if she would ever
know what really ran through his mind. Amanda ran
her fingers across her brow. Her headache was gone.
True to his word, Jeb had driven it away and he had
driven away every thought of Cherie for a time, but
now the demon thoughts were returning to plague her.
Amanda wondered how long Cherie would stay with
them.

The next day Cherie stayed at the house all day,
hovering over Kevin, giving orders to Mrs. Fletcher
and taunting Amanda with biting remarks.

That night Amanda bathed Kevin, knowing Cherie was out on the porch flirting outrageously with Jeb.

When Jeb came home the following day, he slowed the pickup as he approached the house. Cherie was seated in the shade on the corral fence. She climbed down and came toward him, blocking his way. She wore a bright blue halter top and tight-fitting skimpy shorts, and she was even more beautiful than he remembered. She flagged him to a stop and walked around to his open window.

"Hi. I was waiting for you to get home."

Ten

"What do you want, Cherie?"

"Can we talk a few minutes? Get out. I know you're hot."

He climbed out, too aware that they were on the back side of the barn and out of sight of the house or any people. Cherie moved close to him to run her fingers along his arm. "Don't you feel something? Be truthful."

He looked at her wide blue eyes and flawless skin. "You're very beautiful," he said, thinking he would have to be dead not to have some kind of physical response to her attention. "But I'm not interested. I'm a married man, Cherie. Happily married."

"You're not in love."

"Yes, I am," he said evenly.

She shook her head, moving closer to him. "I don't

think you are. You don't act like a man in love. I should know.''

"I've changed and I love Amanda,'' he declared.

"Jeb, I can give you and Kevin so much. Remember how good it was when we made love? I remember exactly. I remember—''

"Cherie, I'm hot, tired and I want to see Amanda and Kevin. I'll see you at dinner.''

Not caring that anger snapped in her blue eyes, he climbed into the pickup and drove past her. He thought about his declarations of love. He had been so set against falling in love again, guarding his broken heart, that he hadn't stopped to really think about his feelings for Mandy. He had told Cherie he was in love with Amanda, but it had been a defensive answer. Not since the wedding had he stopped to sort out his own feelings.

Was he truly in love? he wondered. He remembered Amanda rocking Kevin and the tenderness in her voice. He thought about her beneath him, her softness enveloping him, her green eyes dark with desire. He knew she was a necessary part of his life, and he loved everything about her.

"I love her,'' he said aloud as he strode toward the house. He wanted to storm inside, find her, carry her to bed to make love to her and tell her all night long how he felt.

He looked at the house, lengthening his stride, and then he remembered that Cherie was living with them and how tense Amanda was. He would wait so they could have a special time when he told her.

He ran through what he wanted to do to surprise her. "I love her,'' he whispered to himself again, knowing that he did. Until today he hadn't stopped to acknowledge his feelings. Maybe he had been scared to look at them too closely. Was she as happy as he was? Twice in the throes of passion he had heard her say "I love you," and he hoped she did love him. Amanda had always been truthful with him. Impatience stabbed him.

They could put up with Cherie a little longer, but then Jeb wanted her to go. He wanted to take Amanda on a short trip where he had her all to himself to tell her he loved her. He would get her another ring—one that came with love this time. She hadn't had a honeymoon. She hadn't had several things she should have had.

He would wait and make it special when he said those three words, but right now, just thinking about her and his feelings for her, he wanted her in his arms desperately. He wanted to love and hold her. One thing—when he declared his love, it shouldn't come as any surprise. He knew he acted as in love as any man could.

He reached for the door, wanting to shout her name, grab her and carry her to bed and pour out his feelings, but they had to go to supper soon with Cherie and Kevin.

"Hot day?" Mrs. Fletcher asked as he walked through the kitchen. Kevin sat at the kitchen table coloring a picture, but the moment Jeb entered the room, he slid off his chair and ran to his dad.

"Hottest one yet," Jeb said, swinging Kevin into his arms and feeling another swell of love, this time for his son. "Hi, Kevin," he greeted him, hugging Kevin and relishing his small arms wrapped around his neck as he hugged Jeb in return. Kevin smelled soapy and clean and Jeb knew he was getting him dusty, but he didn't care. It was sheer heaven to come home and have Kevin throw himself into his arms. He shifted his son so he could hold him and talk to him, and Kevin rested one arm around Jeb's neck. "What's been happening here?"

Kevin merely pointed to his coloring book. "Will you color wif me?"

"After I shower," Jeb said, setting Kevin down. "I'm dusty now. I'll bathe and come back." As soon as Jeb stood and started to walk away, Kevin followed him.

Jeb knew he wasn't going to get Mandy to himself for a while because Kevin often tagged along with him around the house. "What did you do today?" he asked Kevin, looking down the hall and into the family room for Mandy, wanting to see her badly.

Maybe he shouldn't wait. Maybe he should just tell her now that he loved her. He debated with himself as he strode down the hall, but he decided to wait, to try to make that moment special.

And then he saw her coming out of Kevin's room with a pair of small jeans in her hands. She saw him and smiled and his insides constricted while heat flashed in him. She wore cutoffs and a T-shirt and was barefoot with her hair caught up in a ponytail. She looked incredible and he ached to scoop her into his arms and carry her to bed.

"Hi," he said, walking up to her and tilting her face up. He saw her quick searching glance and wondered how her day had been, but then her soft lips were beneath his. He knew Kevin was standing beside him, so he straightened up.

"I'm hot and dusty and going to shower." He

looked down at Kevin. "Are you taking a shower with me?"

Kevin shook his head and turned, running back toward the kitchen. Jeb laughed and looked at her. "I wonder how old he'll be before he minds getting a bath."

"When he notices girls, he'll want to bathe."

"Well, that's my case. I'm noticing one right now and I want to bathe with her. I missed you." He picked her up in his arms and she yelped softly.

"Jeb!"

"I know. I'll get you dusty, but that's just a penalty you pay for having a husband who can't wait to get you in his arms." Once again he was torn between telling her right now that he loved her or waiting to make it special. He strode into their bedroom and turned to swing the door shut with his toe. As he did, he glanced down the hall and saw Cherie standing at the end of the hall watching them.

"Jeb," Amanda said as the door closed and he leaned against it, setting her on her feet. "I feel Cherie's presence all the time. It's like she's here with us. I want her out of here."

"I want her out of here, too," he said solemnly, "but I think it's only fair to give her some time with Kevin."

"I don't think it's Kevin who's holding her here," Amanda said quietly.

"If I thought she didn't care about Kevin, I'd run her off the place right now." As Amanda started to move away, Jeb caught her, pulling her roughly against him. "Come here. This is what I've been waiting for since breakfast." Moving back to lean against the closed door, he bent his head to kiss her hungrily, wanting her and knowing he should wait until he showered, but thinking that then he might not be alone. He reached behind him to turn the lock on their bedroom door and then his hand slid to her cutoffs to unfasten them.

"I want you, Mandy," he whispered hoarsely, showering her with kisses, sliding his hand beneath the cutoffs and lace panties. Consumed with desire for her, he couldn't wait, kissing her hard and deep, his hand finding her soft, intimate places.

With a moan of pleasure Amanda melted into his embrace. The stiffness and worry and strain of Cherie being in the house evaporated. Jeb was dusty and sweaty, but she no longer cared. He was shaking with need, kissing her as if their kisses were his first in a year, his hands stroking her and driving every thought out of her head.

She was in his arms, being loved by him, and suddenly the world was right again. He was her man and he was showering her with love. He shoved away her clothing and pulled her T-shirt over her head, tossing it aside.

She wanted Jeb, all his hardness, his strength, his reassurance. She unfastened his jeans and shoved them away, peeling away his briefs and letting them fall around his ankles, wanting him with the same desperate urgency with which he seemed to need her.

He lifted her up and she wrapped her long legs around him and then his shaft slowly filled her. Sensations consumed her in scalding flames, and she clung to him while they moved in unison to a bursting release. "Jeb! My Jeb!" she cried softly, clinging to his broad, strong shoulders.

With ragged breathing, they slowed, and she slid

her legs down his, standing on her own feet. "Now I need that shower, too."

"We'll do that when I get out of these boots," he said with a grin. "I was a man in a hurry."

She rubbed against him with a purr. "I'm glad. It makes me feel wanted."

"You're wanted, all right," he said roughly, "and if you don't quit rubbing against me like that, we'll never get that shower."

"Mandy!" he yelled, struggling to get off a boot while standing with one arm still around her. He stepped away and she looked at him, naked, with his clothes shoved around his ankles while he tried to get off his boots, and she laughed.

"What a sight you are!"

He grinned at her. "You got me in this predicament and it's embarrassing, and if you don't stop laughing at me, I'll take some sweet revenge."

"Phooey!" She laughed as he hobbled to a chair and sat down, struggling to yank off his boots. He looked up at her and grinned.

"Just you wait!"

She turned and rushed to their bathroom to start the shower. In seconds he stepped in with her. "Now. I told you if you kept laughing, I'd get my revenge."

"You can't. We've got to show up at supper, and Kevin will probably come looking for us any minute now."

"Words, words," he said, running his hands over her hips and then up over her rib cage to cup her breasts.

She inhaled swiftly, but caught his wrists. "You don't get your way this time!" She stepped out of the shower swiftly, grabbed a towel and moved away from him.

Watching her, Jeb finished showering, knowing she was right but already wanting her again. Her green eyes sparkled mischievously and he was glad they'd made love because she looked far happier than she had when he had come home.

His mind jumped to where they could go for a delayed honeymoon. Tomorrow he would go into town and look at rings.

While he finished showering, Amanda pulled on a blue-and-white sundress, slipped on sandals and brushed her hair into a ponytail again swiftly. Jeb came out of the shower with only a towel wrapped around his waist. He was dark brown, hard with muscle, tall and lean, and she drew a deep breath at the sight of him. Just looking at him could turn her to jelly. With an effort she tore her gaze away and rushed to leave the room, afraid if he dropped the towel, she would walk right back into his arms.

"Mandy," he said softly.

She turned with her hand on the doorknob.

"You look pretty."

"Thanks. So do you."

He grinned and glanced down at himself. "That's a first, and something I never expected to hear."

"Pretty sexy, cowboy." She laughed and left their bedroom, closing the door behind her.

The next day it was half past six when she returned home from work. Jeb's pickup wasn't in sight, Mrs. Fletcher had asked for three days off, and Amanda knew Kevin was with Jeb. She wondered what Cherie had done by herself all day.

As Amanda opened the back door, she glanced over

her shoulder and saw Kevin riding Popcorn as Jake
led the pinto around the corral. Kevin waved and she
waved in return. She would change and then go join
them. She wondered where Jeb was, but knew that
Jake was capable of taking care of Kevin. She knew
that none of them would leave Kevin in Cherie's care.

She moved through the silent house, wondering if
Cherie was gone, too, but when she passed Cherie's
bedroom, the door was closed, so she figured Cherie
was in her room.

The moment Amanda entered her own bedroom, she
paused, inhaling deeply. It was easy to recognize
Cherie's perfume lingering in the air. Why had Cherie
been in their bedroom?

Annoyed, Amanda unzipped her dress and stepped
out of it, crossing to the closet to hang it up. She
turned, looking at the room that appeared undisturbed,
yet she was certain Cherie had been in it. If she hadn't
have been looking, she might never have noticed, but
she saw a tiny bit of pink under the edge of the bed.
Crossing the room, she bent down, retrieved a bit of
silk and held it up, looking at a pair of pink panties
edged in lace. Amanda turned to ice, because she
wasn't looking at a scrap of her own clothing. It was
Cherie's.

Stunned, she sank down on the edge of the bed. Had
Jeb and Cherie been in here? In the bed she shared
with Jeb? Pain consumed her. How could Jeb have
done that? But she knew instantly. Cherie was female
perfection—physical perfection, at least. How could
he resist her day after day and night after night when
she was being her most charming with him, throwing
herself at him, flirting with him. He would have to be
made of ice to be impervious to her.

Amanda's stomach churned and anger and hurt battled within her. Her marriage was nothing but a paper promise, done for Kevin. Yet Jeb had acted like a man in love.

With shaking hands she flung the panties on the bed and rushed to yank on cutoffs and a T-shirt. She grabbed the panties and charged down the hall, flinging open the door to Cherie's room.

Stretched out in bed, Cherie sat up, her blue eyes widening.

Amanda flung the pink silk onto the foot of the bed. "You left that in our room today."

Cherie's face flushed and she yanked up the panties. "Amanda, I'm sorry," she whispered, looking guilty and smug at the same time. "We—I just—I'm sorry."

"Cherie, why don't you get out? You're not interested in Kevin. You want Jeb back even though he's married to me now."

Eleven

Cherie's eyes narrowed, her expression hardening as she swung her feet to the floor and stood, tossing the panties back onto the bed.

"Jeb loves me whether he'll admit it or not. And face it—what man wouldn't like two women fawning over him?" Cherie smiled at her. "It's like I told you, you haven't lost him, because you never really had him."

"We have a good marriage," Amanda said stiffly, wondering what she had now.

"Do you think if you had come into our house the third month of our marriage like I have yours, that you could have gotten him to show any interest in you?"

The question hurt, and Amanda struggled with her anger. "I want you to go."

"Amanda, you're the one who should leave. Jeb and Kevin and I are the true family. You're standing in the way of Kevin having the family he should have had. If you really loved him, you'd give him up.''

Amanda drew a deep breath, remembering Cherie begging her to take Kevin, telling her she didn't want to see him or hold him after he was born.

"I'm Kevin's mother and the only mother he's ever known. And I'm Jeb's wife and we love each other.''

"When I want to, I can make Jeb happy—make him happier than you'll ever make him. You're the one being selfish, Amanda. If you'd leave, we'd be a family. I'm Kevin's real mother. I'm the woman Jeb truly loves. I can give Jeb the children he wants and you can't. And I can give Jeb and Kevin a life that they'll never know otherwise because I'm making a fortune. Stop thinking of yourself and think of Jeb and Kevin and what I can do for them.''

Her words cut like knives and Amanda wondered if she was standing selfishly in the way, blinded by her own love for Kevin and Jeb. Yet she couldn't forget Cherie's total disregard for Kevin when he was born. She shook her head, hot with hurt and anger.

"You're the one who should pack and go. You're disrupting our lives. You don't really care about Kevin, and the moment you stop showing interest in him, Jeb will lose all interest in you,'' she said.

Cherie glanced at the underwear on the bed. "He won't stop showing interest in me,'' she said slyly. "You're wrong.''

"If Jeb denies he was with you, I'll believe him. And I don't think he was,'' she said, suddenly realizing how easily Cherie could have put the scrap of clothing in their room. Thinking about it, she grew more certain and more angry. "You don't belong here, Cherie, and you're trying to hurt all three of us.''

"Nonsense."

"If I walked out, you wouldn't want to live out here on the ranch with Jeb. You have a career."

"It would sound so good if I had a Texas husband to come back to. I could make my movies and come back here several times a year."

"And what about a mother for Kevin?"

She shrugged. "Children get used to anything. Jeb would take care of him, and when he's older, he can be sent away to school."

"That's a selfish view. Have you ever thought about anyone besides yourself?"

"It doesn't pay to. Except I'm thinking of Jeb now. You know I can make him happier than you can. Look at me. Do you know how many proposals I get a month?"

"Cherie, I've known you all your life. Stop and look at yourself. You're trying to tear up three lives on a whim. All your life you've done as you pleased— I've always known that—but down deep, I always thought there was a basic decency in you. Now I wonder."

Cherie blinked, staring at Amanda while all color drained from her face.

"You get out of my house. I love my son and my husband and you're not going to interfere. You pack and I'll drive you into town now. Our family ties are severed."

Amanda left to go to the corral to find Jake. Her hands were shaking with anger and she took deep breaths, trying to calm herself. Jake saw her and climbed over the fence while Kevin continued riding Popcorn around the corral.

"He's going to be a fine cowboy."

"Well, I hope not this year," she answered lightly. Jake's eyes narrowed and he studied her.

"Something wrong?"

"No. I just wanted to see if you can continue watching Kevin. Cherie's leaving, and I'm driving her into town."

"Want me to take her?" he asked.

She stared at him and thought about it, then shook her head. "No. I think I need to get away by myself for a little while. Jeb will be home before long, won't he?"

"Yep. He's mending a fence."

"I work in town tomorrow. I think I'll just stay at my house in town tonight."

Jake nodded. She passed him and climbed the corral fence to wave at Kevin and blow him a kiss. "Take care of my baby," she said softly.

"I will. Don't you worry."

"Thanks, Jake." She headed toward the house.

"Amanda," Jake said, and she turned. "Whatever happened today, Jeb hasn't been home since early this morning."

"I didn't much think he had, but it's nice to hear. Thanks." She turned and went to the house, wondering how much had shown in her expression and how much Jake had guessed.

She was sending Cherie packing, yet Cherie's words taunted her and hurt. Was she being selfish and standing in the way of Kevin and Jeb having so much more? She could never give Jeb more children and that knowledge hurt deeply.

She waited in the kitchen and then silently helped a white-faced Cherie carry her bags to the car. They rode in silence, and as she drove away from the ranch,

Amanda forgot Cherie's presence. Numb and hurt at the same time, she glanced in the rearview mirror as the home she had grown to love disappeared from view. *Kevin and Jeb were her life.*

"Just take me to the airport. I'm going to Nashville."

Amanda didn't bother answering, but drove to Dallas-Fort Worth International Airport and parked to let Cherie unload her things. Amanda got out to remove Cherie's bags from the trunk. When she slammed it shut and set the bags on the walk, she looked at her cousin. "Goodbye, Cherie."

Cherie turned abruptly and called for an attendant to help with her luggage. Amanda climbed into her car and drove away without looking back. Yet Cherie's perfume stayed in the car and her words lingered in Amanda's mind—words that hurt and worried her. Was she doing the wrong thing in binding Jeb to her in marriage? Was she being selfish with Jeb and Kevin? Particularly with Jeb because she couldn't give him more children.

Lost in her thoughts she drove to her home and let herself into the quiet house that now seemed so small and so terribly empty.

"Jeb, I love you," she said quietly, letting tears come and wondering whether, if she truly loved him, she would let him go.

In early evening at the ranch, Jeb slowed, stopped in front of the garage and climbed out of his pickup. He headed to the house in long strides. As he entered the kitchen, Jake and Kevin looked up. Seated at the table, Kevin was coloring and drinking chocolate milk while Jake sat across from him, nursing a beer.

"We made ourselves at home."

"That's fine," Jeb said, grabbing up Kevin, who had run to greet him. He hugged and kissed Kevin. "How's my boy?"

"Fine. I rode Popcorn all by myself."

"Good for you!" He set Kevin on his feet, and Kevin ran back to sit at the table and drink his chocolate milk and continue coloring.

"Amanda's not home from work yet?"

"Yep. She drove Cherie into town to the airport."

Startled, Jeb paused as he started to take a sip of beer. "Cherie's gone without saying goodbye?"

"Looks as if," Jake drawled, and Jeb glanced at Kevin, who was now looking at one of his picture books. Jeb motioned with his head and Jake followed him into the hall.

"What happened? That's not like either one of them."

Jake shrugged. "Dunno. Amanda said to tell you she's staying in town at her house tonight."

With foreboding, Jeb decided something was wrong. "I'm going to shower. Can you stay that much longer with Kevin?"

"Sure. I can stay all night if you want to go into town to see Amanda."

"Thanks, Jake. I'll give her a call. Have they had time to get there?"

"Yep, they have. Just let me know. I'll be in the kitchen with Kevin."

"Thanks. Get whatever you want to eat."

Jeb headed for his room, closing the door and going straight to the phone to call Amanda. He suspected something bad had happened for her to leave the way she had and to tell Jake she wouldn't be back tonight.

He listened to her phone ring and then got the familiar answering machine. Frustrated and worried, he left a message.

By eight o'clock, he had sent Jake home and he was getting worried about Amanda. Kevin had gone to bed, but Jeb was tempted to get him up and drive into town to look for her. Except he didn't know where to start.

When the phone rang, he grabbed the receiver and said hello. The moment he heard her voice, relief swamped him.

"Jeb, I just got home and heard your message," Amanda said.

"I was worried about you."

"Didn't Jake tell you that I was staying in town?"

"Yes, he did," Jeb answered, thinking she sounded stiff and cool. "What's wrong?"

There was a long silence and his sense of foreboding increased.

"Jeb, I need to think things through."

"What things?" he asked while a dull pain started in his middle. "How about I get Jake to come up and stay with Kevin and I come into town so we can talk? I hate talking over the phone."

"Not tonight. I want some time to myself."

He thought that over, wanting to be with her so he could find out what was troubling her and what had happened today.

"All right. Have dinner with me tomorrow night."

"I don't know. I want to think about our marriage and about Kevin. We rushed into marriage."

"Are you sorry?" he asked stiffly.

"I'll never be sorry," she said softly, and he wondered whether she was crying. Gritting his teeth, he wanted to swear because he needed to be with her.

"I have to stop and look at what we're doing," she said. "There are several of us involved and it's important to do the right thing for Kevin and you as well as me."

"You were pretty sure about Kevin not very long ago."

"I'll talk to you tomorrow evening, Jeb."

"Amanda, don't hang up," he said, and received another long silence.

"Sure you don't want me to come to town? I'd like to."

"Wait until tomorrow, Jeb. I'm going now. Good night."

He heard a click and then he was cut off. "Lady, what's wrong?" he asked the empty room. What had happened here today? he wondered. He went out to the back porch, staring down the road and wondering what was bothering her.

Amanda replaced the receiver gently, wiping at tears and staring at the phone. Cherie's words had shaken her. She didn't think Jeb would ever want to go back to Cherie, but she did think he would someday want a woman who could give him more children. *"You're the one being selfish, Amanda. If you'd leave, we'd be a family. I'm Kevin's real mother. I'm the woman Jeb truly loves. I can give Jeb the children he wants and you can't."*

The words rang in Amanda's mind. Was she being selfish or were they becoming a family? Each time she asked herself that question and thought about the happy times, the intimate moments with Jeb and her deep love for Kevin, she felt that their marriage was right and good. But then when she thought about Jeb wanting more children, a cloud darkened their future because she couldn't have any. He had blithely said they could adopt, but did he really feel that way?

She spent a sleepless night and found no satisfying answers to her questions.

Then at work she forgot her own problems as she talked with her patients, tested their hearing and fitted hearing aids. But when the day was over and she was driving home, excitement began to curl inside her, because at seven she would see Jeb. He had called her twice today, talking briefly each time. During the day he had taken Kevin to his mother's and she was keeping him for the next two days.

Amanda's pulse raced as she dressed. She wanted to see Jeb and be with him. She loved him, but she had to know his feelings because she didn't want to stand in the way of his happiness. Too well, she was aware that he had never told her he loved her. Yet he acted like a man in love, she reminded herself, thinking about their moments together.

Slipping into sleeveless, deep blue cotton dress, she pinned her hair on top of her head, put on a gold chain bracelet and decided she was ready. As she stepped into high-heeled sandals, the doorbell rang.

While her heart missed beats, she hurried through the house, opened the door and stepped back.

"Hi," Jeb said quietly, coming into the house and closing the door behind him. He was devastatingly handsome in his dark suit and crisp white shirt and dark tie. More than ever now that he was standing in front of her, she wanted to fling herself into his arms.

As she stared into fathomless dark pools, her breath caught. Tension sizzled between them, like tiny explosions in the crackling air, and she couldn't move.

"I missed you. Why did you go?" he asked.

"There are some things we need to discuss."

He reached out then and touched her, his hand sliding around her waist, and her heart thudded violently. Desire blossomed and she wanted to be in his arms. She was aching to hold him and be wrapped in his embrace and forget every worry nagging her.

"I have some things to tell you," he said solemnly. "I was going to take you to dinner and then come back and tell you, but I think I've waited too long already."

He drew her close and her hands were on his upper arms, feeling his smooth lightweight suit jacket and his hard muscles beneath it.

He leaned down to kiss her, his tongue sliding deeply into her mouth, stroking her, awakening too many feelings and needs as she moaned softly and trembled and wrapped her arms around his neck to kiss him in return. How could she walk away and give him up? He acted as though he were in love, and she wanted him so badly.

He pulled back to place his fingers against her throat, studying her. "Your pulse is racing," he said in a husky voice.

"You do that to me."

Something flickered in the depths of his eyes. "Look in my pocket. I brought something for you."

Mystified, she reached into his coat pocket and brought out a ring box, remembering the last time he had done the same thing. She already had a wedding ring and they were married, so, even more puzzled, she stared at the box. Opening it, she saw an emerald surrounded by diamonds.

"Jeb!" she gasped, surprised and uncertain.

Taking the ring from her, he held her right hand. "This is for the love we have now. I love you, Mandy. I love you with all my heart. You're the woman of my dreams, and this time, I'm damn sure."

"Jeb!" she cried, unable to talk as tears stung her eyes and she stared at him. "You're certain how you feel?"

"Absolutely," he said. "And I've waited too long to tell you."

"Jeb, that's why I left," she said quietly, looking at the deep green stone. "I can't give you more children and I know you want some."

"Mandy, we talked about that. We can adopt. You adopted Kevin and it's very good, isn't it?"

"Yes, but am I cheating you and Kevin both—"

"Oh, hell. Lady, I don't want to live without you. Last night was hell. Don't ever leave me again. If we can't adopt, I don't care. I have you and Kevin and that's my family and it's wonderful. I love you and I want you. You're my wife and I love you, now and always."

She let go of her worries. "I gave you your chance," she whispered, standing on tiptoe and pulling his head down to her. "I missed you incredibly," she said, kissing him and sliding her hands beneath his suit coat to shove it off his shoulders. Her heart pounded with joy that she had Jeb back. It was right and good, and she could get rid of doubts and go back to the life she loved on the ranch.

Her fingers fumbled with his belt and unbuckled it while he tugged down the zipper of her dress. While cool air spilled over her shoulders, he walked her back toward her bedroom. Clothes fell through the house until they reached the bed, and he shoved away the last scrap of lace and she peeled away his briefs to toss them aside.

Jeb picked her up and gently placed her on the bed, leaning over her to shower kisses down her stomach, trailing lower to her inner thighs. "I love you, I love you," he whispered over and over, kissing her, his hands stroking her, one hand moving between her legs while his other hand circled her nipple.

Amanda moaned with pleasure, winding her fingers in his hair and then caressing him, sliding her hands over his muscled back down to his firm buttocks. She sat up to take his thick shaft in her hands and stroke and kiss him until he moved her away to kiss her.

"Jeb, I love you," she whispered, and he kissed her, finally pulling back to wind his fingers in her hair and draw his other hand lightly across her lips.

"I love you, lady. I can't ever tell you how much I love you, but I'll spend a lifetime showing you. I'm sorry I didn't tell you sooner."

"Oh, Jeb!" she cried, joy and desire shaking her as she flung herself against him and kissed him hard and long.

Finally he moved between her legs, ready, devouring her with his heated gaze as he lowered himself into her, filling her and moving slowly in a sweet torment that drove her wild.

They moved together, Amanda's hips arching to meet him until release came and Jeb shuddered. "Mandy, I love you," he cried, and kissed her hungrily.

She clung to him, in ecstasy from their loving and from his words. They still moved together, slowing, trying to catch their breaths, coming back to earth to kiss and fondle each other leisurely now.

Later, as Jeb held her close against him, she looked again at her beautiful new ring. "I didn't know whether you loved me or not."

"How could you not know?" he asked, frowning. "I should have told you before now, but I didn't stop to think about what I felt until Cherie forced the issue, and then I wanted the right moment to tell you."

"The right moment?" she asked, frowning and rising up on an elbow to look at him. The sheet was tucked beneath her arms and draped across his hips as she stared at him. "*Any* moment is the right moment. How long ago did you decide you loved me?"

"I didn't want to tell you while Cherie was there. You know the evenings were tense. I wanted a special time and place and I wanted to get you a ring—"

"Oh, Jeb, all you needed to do was say it, just say the three little words! It would have been as thrilling whether it had been one night last week or now. It doesn't matter what or when—I just want to know how you feel."

He frowned and pushed wavy tendrils of her red hair away from her face. "I figured you'd know how I felt. Don't I act like a man in love?"

"Yes, you do, but you also act like a man in lust. How was I to know which one you felt?"

"Both, lady. Damn well both. I'm sorry, Mandy, if I should have told you sooner. Is that why you left last night?"

"That and worrying about being unable to give you children."

"Will you stop with that? Why don't we start adoption proceedings right now and then you'll never worry about that again."

She smiled and framed his face with her hands. "I don't think I'm ever going to worry about it again, anyway," she said, leaning down to kiss him, her heart overflowing with love.

Epilogue

Jeb sat with his long legs stretched out, his booted feet propped on the porch rail. In one hand he had a glass of iced tea. With his other, he reached out to take Amanda's hand. Summer shadows were long across the mowed green lawn as evening set in. Mrs. Fletcher sat knitting in the shade of an oak while seven-year-old Kevin tossed a ball to redheaded four-year-old Brad. Toddling back and forth between them was their two-year-old sister, black-haired Emily.

"Think I ought to rescue Emily? Those boys aren't paying any attention to her."

"She's happy just to be with them. That's the way women are with their menfolk around," Amanda replied, and Jeb grinned.

"Come sit on my lap."

As she moved over to his lap, he put his feet on the floor, holding her and stroking her arm. "A seven-year-old, a four-year-old and a two-year-old. It's pretty nice, isn't it?''

"It's the best, and so are you,'' she whispered, patting his face and leaning close to kiss him.

When the roar of a bike interrupted them, she looked around. "Here comes Jake to say goodbye.''

"Yeah, to say goodbye again. He left four months after we married, came back a year later and now he's leaving again. I wonder how long before he's back.''

She stood and Jeb came to his feet, draping his arm around her shoulders. "What drives him, Jeb, to keep moving? He's a wonderful man and half the women in this county are in love with him.''

"I don't know. I've never asked and he's never said.''

They walked out to the gate and Kevin and Brad came running, Emily slowly toddling along behind them. Jeb picked up Brad, and when Emily reached them, Amanda scooped her into her arms.

Jake slowed the Harley and cut the motor, joining them to greet the children first. Jake hunkered down to look at Kevin. "I'll miss you and I promise to come back to see you.'' He stood and swung Kevin into his arms to hug him. Then when he set him down, he said, "Be a good big brother, okay?''

"Yes, sir.''

He picked up Brad. "And you be a good little brother,'' Jake said, hugging him.

"Yes, sir,'' Brad said, hugging Jake in return.

Jake set him down and looked at Emily. "And you be a good little sister,'' he said, winking at her. She smiled and wrapped her arms around Amanda's neck.

"You take care of him, because he needs some care,'' Jake said to Amanda, hugging her lightly, and she hugged him, kissing his cheek.

"You take care of yourself," she said. "There are a lot of ladies here who don't want to see you go."

He grinned and looked at Jeb, offering his hand. "You know I'll be back."

"I hope so. I'll miss you and my horses will miss you."

"Take care of your family and yourself. 'Bye, Mrs. Fletcher," he called and she waved. Jake turned and got on his bike and with a roar drove down the road toward the highway. Wind blew his long black hair and he didn't look back as he rounded a curve and disappeared from sight. The boys ran back to playing ball and Emily wriggled to get down and join them. Jeb and Amanda strolled back to the porch and quiet once again settled.

"I've got a good idea," Jeb drawled. "While Mrs. Fletcher watches the kids, come here and let me show you something." He took her hand and led her into the house.

"What are you doing?" she asked, and then laughed as he pulled her inside and closed the door, leaning against it and hauling her into his embrace.

"Let me show you how fast a Texas cowboy can get something done once he puts his mind to it."

"His mind my eye!" she said, laughing and wrapping her arms around his neck. "All right, cowboy, do your stuff."

Jeb pulled her close to kiss her. Amanda closed her eyes, standing on tiptoe, her heart filled with joy for this tall Texas cowboy and the wonderful family and love they had.

*   *   *   *   *

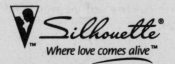

Look in the back pages of
all June Silhouette series books to find an
exciting new contest with fabulous prizes!
Available exclusively through Silhouette.

Don't miss it!

Where love comes alive™

P.S. Watch for details on how you can meet
your favorite Silhouette author.